I0647716

Eastern Orchid

Eastern Orchid

ISBN: 978-0-9966565-5-9 Jasmaya Productions and Publications Tucson, Arizona, 85747

JASMAYA
Productions & Publications
The Eyes of Independent Publishing

BOOK ONE

CHAPTER ONE

The campus was buzzing with the news the Americans would be arriving in a few minutes. The students who'd be guiding the American students sat in the auditorium of the Uzbekistan International University speaking in soft tones and watching the Dean and President of the university trying to remain calm, but their smoking and pacing illustrated they were nervous. Shahknoza, Orchid's best friend's leg jumped up and down and she chewed her gum making squishing sounds. Orchid placed her slender fingers on Shahknoza's knee.

"Shakhnoz, stop that, you're making me nervous."

Shahknoza moved her first and third fingers in circles until the back door opened and everyone turned around. Shahknoza elbowed Orchid in the side, causing her to bend over in pain.

"Oh my god Orchid. Look at him. He looks like one of the men in the movies we've seen"

Orchid's mouth fell open and she touched her chest to make sure her heart hadn't fallen to the floor because she felt it beating in her feet. What made it worse was he took off his dark glasses, stared at Orchid, and making no sound, said "hi" with his mouth. Shahknoza elbowed Orchid again.

"He saw you and said hello. Didn't you see him?" Orchid rubbed her side.

"You're always exaggerating Shahknoz. He was looking at all of us".

Shahknoz stood like all of the students who'd been selected and followed the other students down the aisle.

"You're silly and I'm not exaggerating. The tall one with the blond hair is mine, and the short one with the big tits is yours".

They walked up the auditorium steps and approached the American students who waited for them, each student wearing a colored tag, which matched the Uzbekistan students colored tag. Walking by him and towards Lena, who she'd be paired with for the year, he raised his glasses and said hello in Uzbek. Orchid dropped her head and inhaling the cologne he wore, her knees shaking, and refusing to look at him, stammered hello, and gave her hand to Lena, who reached out and hugged her, giving her a kiss on the cheek. Orchid looked at Shahknoza shaking Miriam's hand, who she'd been paired with, and then she noticed Shahknoza's back stiffen as Miriam hugged her. Turning Miriam, Shahknoza winked at Orchid, mouthing these

4

Americans are different, then raised her chin towards Salim, who Orchid couldn't see, but Shahknoza could see, was looking towards her, through dark glasses concealed his eyes.

Classes stopped and students came from their classrooms to look at the new American arrivals as they passed, going to the cafeteria. She heard the students say as they walked by "look at him, his hair looks like a mop, or coils". Siroj, who walked with Salim, and was paired with him, slowed a bit and catching Orchid's eyes, pointed to Salim's hair. Orchid, her face crimson, nodded and glanced at Salim, taller than all of them, probably six foot three, with a full trimmed mustache and beard, his face slow but steady, his head moving and taking in everything, skin like fresh honey, carrying two instrument cases, a flute and a trumpet, smiling at everyone and humming. Orchid knew, at that moment, something had occurred which she had to hide, because it frightened her.

They stopped at tables in the cafeteria and Siroj, Shahknoza, Salim, Lena and Miriam sat together. The cafeteria workers brought them tea, which Lena smelled before drinking, causing Shahknoza to kick Orchid under the table, and Miriam and Salim to turn their heads towards her. Salim raised his glasses and frowned at Lena, who stared into her tea.

"I like the tea Siroj. Is this what you drink this time of year?"

Siroj opened his mouth and closed it, unable to answer. Orchid warmed her fingers on the cup.

"We drink this on cool days. In the summer we drink something like this, but with ice. It's from the mulberry trees."

Her voice bounced inside her head and Shahknoza started rambling, talking about the mulberry trees, this time of year, and everyone laughed because she was speaking so fast and mixing English with Uzbek, that everyone at the table could only understand every other word. Miriam took Shahknoza's hand.

"Shahknoza, please slow down. I only understood half of what you said"

Siroj thumbed the table.

"I only understood half too. What language are you speaking, Uzbeklish?"

Shahknoza let out a loud cackle and everyone laughed again. The other tables looked at them, but they didn't care. They all spoke at the same time, mostly in English, but sometimes using Uzbek, or Russian words.

In those few moments, and exchanges, Orchid learned Lena spoke Russian and German, Miriam Farsi, Arabic, and Salim French, Spanish, Italian, Portuguese, Russian, Arabic, and Uzbek which he'd been studying for two years. Siroj sat between she and Salim, and whenever Salim would address Orchid directly, Siroj would interrupt. Orchid said "ouch" because Shahknoza, noticing what Siroj was doing, kicked her again. Orchid refused to look at her because she knew, what Shahknoza knew; Siroj was in love with her, and he sensed what she felt for Salim. Shahknoza, using her native Tatar, which she'd taught to Orchid, and which she knew only the two of them understood, said "come with me to the toilet", and they stood up. Orchid smiled at Siroj and the others.

"We'll be right back. We're going to the ladies' room".

Siroj and the others nodded, and she felt Salim's eyes, behind the dark glasses looking at her body as she stood. Shahknoza took Orchid's hand and dragged her to the bathroom.

Once inside she jumped into the air.

"Did you see that? Oh my god, he's so beautiful I could pour him into my tea and drink him. And did you see Siroj cutting him off every time he tried to speak to you? He loves you Orchid, he loves you and he didn't show it until now. I thought men were stupid but he's not so stupid because he sees Salim, beautiful Salim is interested in you and he's jealous. What are you going to do Orchid? What are you going to do? He loves you. And Salim speaks some Uzbek so we have to be careful what we say. And they all speak Russian so when our English doesn't work we can still communicate. And did you see Miriam looking at Siroj? She likes the way he looks and that rude one smelling the tea as if something was wrong with it? Oh my god Orchid, isn't this wonderful?"

Orchid leaned against the sink and covered Shahknoza's mouth.

"You think too much Shahknoz. We're just meeting them and you've already created a story. I keep telling you that you need to be a writer with your stories. I don't see any of that".

Shahknoza put her hands on her hips.

"Don't play stupid with me Orchid. I know you and I know you saw Siroj and that woman looking at him. Are you jealous? Hmmmm. I know you. You're playing it cool because you like that honey dipper with the beautiful hair and the big hands. Hmmmm. I know you Orchid. You don't fool me."

The door opened and Miriam and Lena entered. Orchid pointed to the stalls and she and her best friend pretended to wash their hands while they waited for the American young women to finish. Shahknoza mouthed words and winked at Orchid, who pretended to kick her.

Exiting the lavatory, Orchid and Shahknoza halted, hearing a trumpet in the hallway between the lavatory and the hall. The toilet's cleaning woman sat with her eyes closed, her toothless smile beaming, and arms folded as she swayed to the melody dancing off the cafeteria ceiling. The trumpet played to I'll Take You To The Sky a poem by Muhammad Yusuf and sung by Yulduz Usmanova, which was a hit in Tashkent because it spoke of a man's undying love and devotion for a woman. The two women stepped from the hall and saw Salim standing, his body in a hardened line, the trumpet balanced straight in front of his face, with his eyes closed, playing along and through the song. Other students accompanied him with their voice, and as the song ended, he continued playing, and people stood and sang two more choruses before stopping, then stood and clapped for Salim who held his horn in the air, then turned to orchid and bowed, offering his trumpet to her, and lifting his dark glasses so that she could see his eyes. Orchid's face burned and she bumped into Shahknoza as she tried to run back into the ladies' room, knocking her friend down and hitting Lena with the door when rushing inside. Bending over the sink she tossed handfuls of cold water on her face, shaking her head throwing water across the room, and opening one eye, she saw Lena rubbing her arm, Miriam watching her with wide eyes and Shahknoza gagging and trying to hold in her laughter.

"What happened out there? You came through that door like something spooked you".

Miriam approached Orchid who stopped her with a raised hand.

"I was lightheaded and I thought I might faint. I'm sorry if I hurt you Lena"

Lena rubbed the purple spot growing on her arm.

"It's ok. The next time just squat and hold your head down. You'll feel better quickly"

Miriam took some Neosporin from her purse and rubbed it on Lena's arm. Shahknoza took a handful of paper towels and rubbed some on Orchid's neck and the others on her face.

"Have you cooled down now? Do you feel better? Shall I wet them and place them in other places?

Orchid snatched the paper towels from Shahknoza's hand and straightened her body upward.

"Shut up Shahknoz. Look I'm all wet".

Shahknoza smacked Orchid on her bottom.

"I bet"

The four women left the bathroom and walked to the table. Siroj sat alone, his eyes in a slit with a closed mouth and flaring nostrils.

"If you're looking for the pied piper he left with a group of music students. I guess he's serenading someone else".

Lena and Miriam sat looking around the cafeteria which was now almost empty, wondering what Siroj has said because they didn't speak Uzbek. Shahknoz translated into Russian.

"What did Salim do?"

Shahknoz stood and mimicked playing a trumpet. Lena and Miriam arched their heads and laughed.

"He did that in the airport in San Francisco and he was joined by some French musicians. It turned into a jam session. Big fun. We loved it. Music needs no words"

Siroj thumbed his nose.

"I guess not. I'll see you ladies later. I need to stop something before it gets out of hand"

Head up and neck sticking forward, Siroj walked like a soldier across the green towards the administration building. Miriam touched Shahknoza with her elbow.

"Where do you think he's going?"

Shahknoza pointed to Orchid.

"To get his rival out of the way"

The four women took a few steps but were halted by an older woman standing in front of them.

"As-Salaam-Alaikum. My name is Petna, Duranova. Orchid Zaynitdinova, my son is

15

interested in you and I want to speak to your parents. May I please have your family's

number?"

Orchid bowed to the older woman and gave her a

phone number and an address. Another woman

approached Shahknoza and did the same. The two

North American women stood saucer eyed as the

two women were approached by four more mothers.

Lena linked arms with them as they walked.

"Is that how it's done? The sons send their mothers

to ask about women they're interested in and then

they go to the girls, get their info and check out the

families?"

Orchid and Shahknoza's heads answered her

questions. Lena's face almost touched Shahknoza's.

"But you don't even know these guys".

Shahknoza looked straight ahead, looking for other mothers.

"It doesn't matter. If our parents' approve of the guy's family, and him, we'll accept their decision and marry him. It's a bit different for me because I'm Tatar, and I already have a boyfriend and we're going to get married after we graduate. I'd still abide by my parents' wishes though if it came to that".

Lena stopped walking.

"That's an arranged marriage. This is the 20th century. What about love?"

Miriam pulled the group along, scowling at Lena.

"Statistics show arranged marriages last longer than romantic marriages because there's no pretense involved Lena. You should know this already. Didn't you attend the seminars?"

Lena fluffed her hair and kept pace with the group, which headed towards a crowd moving to the music coming from inside the building. It was a full orchestra. Miriam moved her shoulders.

"That's Grover Washington's Winelight. They're cooking".

Orchid and Shahknoza froze.

"Cooking?"

Miriam used her hands to mimic stirring a pot.

"It means sounding good. The musicians are playing well together like making good food".

Lena chuckled and Miriam rolled her eyes at her. Getting to the doorway, the students moved aside allowing the foreigners to walk inside with the Uzbek young women. Lena spoke into Shahknoza's ear.

"Why'd they move aside for us?"

"They're being polite because you're guests in our country"

"How'd they know we're not from here?"

Shahknoza thumped Lena's pale breasts.

"No Uzbek girl would walk around with her a blouse cut that low and her breasts showing. We're more modest".

Lena pulled up her top.

"My goodness. What is this the Victorian age?"

The young women went inside and saw Salim standing in front of an orchestra comprised of Uzbek students, with a dark haired oval faced reed bodied director. They moved to the music and wrote on music paper and the band played. Uzbek musicians soloed to the James Brown style funky beat. The director raised his hand to lower the orchestra's volume, then lifted his violin and began

19

to improvise. Salim conducted the orchestra, having them ease up the volume with the violinists playing, making crescendos, swirls, twists until the perspiring director made a screeching run, his hair flying into the air, and Salim repeated the same run on his trumpet and launched into his solo, eyes closed. The conductor moved the band with Salim until they reached a crescendo and stopped. The orchestra stood and applauded with the listeners. The director passed out the music sheets to the different instruments, explaining to them they'd have to read in groups, and giving them one read down of the music, and practicing the rhythm with the drummer, started to count down the beat when Orchid asked if she could play the traditional Uzbek drum, the Doira. Miriam asked if she could play violin and the director left the room and returned with a violin, which he handed to her and then pulled up a chair for her to sit with the violins. A drummer took the pause to ask about the rhythm so Salim picked up a tambourine and played the rhythm as he walked to where the drummer sat with Orchid holding the Doira next to him and Shahknoza held the bracelets, called the zings. They played the rhythm together for a few minutes, with Orchid and Shahknoza adding the Uzbek rhythms. Salim pulled his glasses down, allowing Orchid to see his eyes. Dropping hers, she rolled her fingers on the center of the drum. Shahknoza jingled the bracelets. The director and Miriam were discussing the violin parts, Miriam making quick notations on five separate music sheets when Salim returned to the front where the director stood. The director counted off the rhythm, starting the drummer, Orchid and Shahknoza first, then brought in each section of the orchestra, as Salim played the melody. The band jammed for one hour, each first chair taking a solo. Orchid watched the students dancing outside, around the sides of the auditorium, and behind the director and conductor. She and Salim head a gaze, her fingers and hands moving with his solo, body, and when he wasn't soloing and playing a part, until the music stopped, and everyone cheered again. The band members slapped fives, the putting their instruments away, filed out, with Salim, Miriam, Shahknoza and Orchid being asked to stay. Once the musicians had left the room, the conductor jumped into the air, then landing, lifted Salim and spun him around.

"Where have you been all my life? I've been wanting to play some type of jazz but we have to play traditional music. My God that was wonderful and I'm delighted. We must do this again".

Salim fingered his trumpet.

"I'll play as much as I can, but I'm a medical student studying surgery with Dr. Abdusatarova".

The conductor spread his arms in the air and spun around.

"Do you know who she is?"

Salim opened his mouth and closed it.

"Yes, she's"

The director jackknifed in laughter.

"She's Orchid's aunt. You'll be studying with her aunt. It's a small world isn't it?"

Shahknoza pinched Orchid on the butt but Orchid didn't react. Salim extended his hand to Orchid.

"I'm honored to meet again the niece of a world renown surgeon. She's beyond famous. I knew there was something special about you and I've only seen part of it with your languages and musical ability. I'm sure there's much more".

Shahknoza pinched Orchid again.

"She speaks Russian, Uzbek, Tatar, Farsi, Turkish, English, plays the Doira, piano and is number one in the diplomatic university. Today she had four men ask for her hand but she hasn't selected any of them yet. Her father is the head of the engineering university and her mother was the first female head of the music department in the country, her uncle is a famous journalist and"

"Shahknoz!"

Orchid placed her hand over Shahknoza's mouth and Shahknoz bit her finger. The group laughed and the director extended his hand to Miriam.

"And who beith you, who stroketh the strings of my heart?"

Miriam placed her hand over the director's hand and gulped loud enough for everyone to hear.

"Miriam, and what be your good your name sir?"

The director tried to smooth down the unwilling curls of his mane.

"I'm Yizod Juraeva. Your humble servant"

Miriam crossed her legs and color crept into her face when the director kissed her hand. She pulled it away, keeping her eyes on him and rubbed her blouse with an open palm.

"Where's Lena?"

They all scanned the room for Lena. Miriam rubbed her palms together, and Salim moved the valves on his horn then placed it in its case.

"We'll go look for her. Isn't she rooming with you, Shahknoza?"

Shahknoza, watching Miriam and the director released her focus on them and gave her attention to Salim.

"Yes she is, and we better find her because she doesn't know where it is".

Orchid clapped her hands breaking the director's spell on Miriam.

"Miriam, I'm going to the dorm, are you coming?"

The director coughed.

"I need her to help me with these charts. I'll show her where you stay Orchid and make sure she gets there safely"

Shahknoza giggled,

"I'm sure you will doctor. Let's go. I'm hungry again".

Miriam hugged Salim and whispered he's the one in his ear. Salim nodded and followed Orchid and Shahknoza from the music hall.

Orchid walked on Salim's left side, and Shahknoza on his right, and they moved across the campus to Shahknoza singing a love song in Tatar about two lovers who knew from the first moment that they met, that they were in love, but danced around each other. Her hands moved at the wrists, and with each step her hips and shoulders swayed. Orchid's head was pulled towards Shahknoza's voice, movements, and Salim striding to the song's rhythm. She and his hand brushed, lingered, rubbed, then settled into a motion guided by Shahknoza's singing. Shahknoza voice trailed away when a tall barrel chested moon faced guy with cheek bones so high that his eyes were barely visible and shoulder length hair stepped in front of her. Shahknoza smoothed down her dress, shook her hair, and with eyes batting, and speaking to him in Tatar, explained they were going to their dorms, then placed an open palm on the young man's chest. The slits for eyes opened, and gold rimmed teeth showed. He reached for Salim's hand and nodded to Orchid.

"Hello Salim. I'm Yusuf Abdullaeva, your new roommate".

Shahknoza stammered and Orchid stepped towards Yusuf.

"How can you be his roommate when he's with Siroj?"

Yusuf moved his thumb up and down.

"I have no idea. Yes, I do. The only way this could happen is if Siroj requested a change. I know he did because all Salim's luggage is in my room".

Shahknoza cackled and her head moved from side to side.

"He's good. You live across campus in the athletic dorm. Siroj, Siroj, Siroj"

Orchid looked up at Salim's stone face.

"You'll have quite a walk to get to the medical school. I'm sorry, it has nothing to do with you"

Salim's neck muscles bulged.

"I'm in good shape. It's all good"

Yusuf flexed a muscle.

"You better be if you want to play soccer with me".

Salim flexed his arm.

"I'll take that challenge, but you're basically a pro aren't you? I saw your picture and name on the national team".

Yusuf humbly lowered his head.

"For all practical purposes. I promised my dad I'd finish college and when I do I'll play professionally. Probably abroad because I've already got offers. My young bride and I will be seeing the world".

Shahknoza covered her mouth and placed her hand on Yusuf's chest again. Looking around, he lifted her hand to his lips and placed it again on his chest. Orchid wagged her finger at them.

"You two better stop that".

Shahknoza, glancing at the people walking by and in the distance, removed her hand. Yusuf reached for her hand.

"You're my heart Shahknoz, I'm going to marry you and I don't care what they think. Plus, we're Tatar and they're always going to say something bad about us".

Orchid noticed Salim's eyes narrow puzzled look. Yusuf wrapped his arm around Salim's shoulders.

"Walk with me to our room and I'll tell you about minorities in Uzbekistan, especially the Tatar. We're the direct descendants of Genghis Khan which makes us different and often misunderstood"

The two men walked away leaning into each other and talking. Orchid covered her mouth and pointed at Shahknoza.

"Shahknoz, calm yourself. Your legs are shaking"

Shahknoza pulled her legs together.

"Every day it gets harder to wait until we graduate Orchid. He kissed me and I felt it all over and I dripped. It's happening now. Is that normal?"

Orchid hooked her arm in her friend's and they headed towards their dorm.

"I don't know. That's never happened to me. We'll have to ask one of those village women who doesn't mind talking".

Shahknoza halted their walking.

"You didn't feel something when your hands touched? And what about when he played to you? You didn't get hot Orchid? Your juices didn't flow?"

Orchid brushed the passion starting to drip from her eyes.

"Oh, is that what you mean? Yes, it flowed, and it frightened me. I thought my visitor was coming, and I've been uncomfortable down there because my panties are wet. I don't know if it's normal but it happened to both of us. Let's go talk to Fatima the village woman who cleans the rooms. She'll tell us the truth".

She tried to leave but Shahknoza held her arm.
"And what are you going to do about Salim, Orchid? It's love at first sight?"
Orchid covered her heart.
"I don't know Shahknoz. I guess I'll just wait and see what happens. Now let's go, I want to change, then find Fatima before she leaves for the day."

Giggling, and arm in arm, the two young women skipped across the campus. Arriving at the dorms, they walked down the dorms sage smelling basement steps to the rooms which Fatima occupied during the day. Fatima, sipping from her smoking thermos, loosened and retied her head scarf, and gave them a toothless grin.

As-salaam-Alaikum my daughters. I knew I'd be seeing one of you today. I thought it would only be you Shahk Shahk"

The two young women bowed to the curve eyed toothless shredded spaghetti faced woman and kissing her on the cheeks, smelled a bit of the rice wine everyone knew she mixed with her tea.

"God is good for bringing you both here safely. I guess you came to ask if you were damaged in your roommate's scandal".

She pointed to two small stools where Orchid and Shahknoza sat, watching as Fatima poured them some tea from a different thermos. She handed them a smoking cup.

"I see from your faces you don't know yet"

Fatima rose from her stool, her white cotton dress below her knees and easing her small feet into slippers, took short steps across the floor and pulled a folded eight and a half white sheet of paper from her handbag hanging on the door.

"Look,"

The two young women unfolded the paper.

Shahknoza pulled her hair.

"Oh my God, it's Lena".

Orchid took deep breaths.

"And she's naked. Fatima, who took this?"

Fatima snatched the paper from them and tore it into small pieces.

"it doesn't matter who took it. What's important is what they did with it. The picture was posted in this dorm and in the men's medical student's dorm.

Your friend saw it and dragging her bags she left the campus in a taxi".

Shahknoza began walking in a circle.

"Where'd she go?"

Fatima returned to her stool and finished her tea.

"To the airport"

Shahknoza squinted her left eye at Fatima.

"How do you know all this?"

Fatima took their tea cups still full of tea, poured them into a sink, rinsed out the cups and placed them on a shelf behind her before grabbing her bag from the door.

"Because my son took her. He's the one with the taxi always parked out front".

Raising her head, she sniffed the air.

"You two smell like passion, but you didn't walk different when you walked in here so I know you haven't done anything. You have questions though.

God has given me gifts to know these things, so I'll

answer your question before you ask. Women run

like water and men squirt in short spurts like water

from streams. It's normal so don't worry. When you

get married you'll feel the squirts inside you. Now

leave, I want to say my prayers before I go home.

These Western girls don't know our ways and it's

your responsibility to teach them. Go."

Orchid and Shahknoza held hands walking through

the dorm removing the picture of a naked Lena.

Pulling down the last picture on the door of her

room, Orchid moved her face close to it.

"Shahknoz, what is that on the table beside the

bed?"

Shahknoz peered at the picture, then held it up to

the light.

"it looks like a ring with a serpent on it".

Orchid put both fists on her hips.

"And who wears a ring with a serpent on it?"

Shahknoza thumbed her nose.

"The four guys from the serpent society"

Orchid flicked her thumb nail against her top teeth.

"And Siroj is one of the four".

The two women left the dorm after changing and showering, then trotting, arrived at the men's medical dorm. Walking around the side of the building, they stood outside a smaller building and looking inside it, searched the faces of the medical students sitting at tables, smoking, drinking tea and soft drinks, playing backgammon, card games and watching soccer on the television.

"Looking for someone?"

They spun around hearing Siroj's voice. He smashed out his cigarette and blew the smoke into the air. Orchid smacked her hands together.

"Did you do that to Lena?"

Siroj moved around them and placed his hand on the building's door knob.

"No, but I know who did"

Shahknoza kicked dirt on Siroj's shoes.

'Tell us who did it. If it wasn't you, there are only three other people who could have done something so vile. Whoever did it ruined that girl and she left the country".

Siroj opened the door.

"She shouldn't have been acting like a whore. This isn't America. She wasn't here one complete day and she already slept with someone. Imagine what she would have been like after a year. You should be glad you weren't closer to her or people would be whispering about you too. Tatar girl".

Orchid took Shahknoza's hand, placing it under her arm, trying to calm her friend's crimson face which had twisted into a snarl.

"We don't care what they'd say because we'd know it wasn't true. Why don't you all say something to whoever had sex with her and took the picture? Muslim men aren't supposed to sleep with infidel women and that makes whoever did bad".

Siroj opened the door.

"We all give into temptation sometimes and God forgives us. We're still not as bad as her".

Closing the door, he waved to the two women and said something which made the men inside laugh and point at Lena's naked picture hanging next to the television.

Orchid and Shahknoza locked arms as they treaded across the campus. Orchid could hear Shahknoz, as she called her sniffling.

"Don't cry Shahknoz, we don't want them to see you and give them the satisfaction of knowing they've hurt you"

Shahknoza wiped her eyes with her Venus palm. "Men are cruel and insensitive"
Orchid ignored the small groups of girls whispering as they passed.
"Women are worse Shahknoz. Men can't get inside the women's dorms so some women had to post that picture. Look at these bitches whispering. Some of them cover their heads but not their asses behind closed doors, and I bet their knees are raw".

Shahknoz spit in some of the groups directions and heard laughs.

"If they say something to me Orchid, I'm going to slam them. They act as if the picture was of me".

They noticed the director and Miriam approaching them and when the director and Miriam stopped in front of them, Orchid could see Miriam's red nose and eyes. She'd been crying. The director chest rose as he inhaled and lit his pipe.

"I guess you've seen the picture."

Shahknoza touched Miriam's hand and Miriam held hers. The director switched into Tatar.

"The Dean came to the auditorium and lectured Miriam on the values of a Muslim country as if she'd done something. He was very accusatory. I did everything I could to keep from laughing because I know he's sleeping with the Dean of the medical school who's married to an old man. What a hypocrite. Playing Muslim. How disgusting".

41

Miriam put on her dark glasses.

"You don't have to speak in a language I don't understand to protect my feelings, I understand American women have a bad reputation and people think we're loose. It comes from the movies and Lena confirmed that stereotype. I wonder what he'd say if he knew my mother's Jewish?"

Shahknoza squeezed Miriam's hand.

"Shhh. Don't say that so loud. People will hate you".

Miriam bit her bottom lip.

'I'm sure they will and I don't care, but I'll keep it to myself because it's no one's business. I guess the Muslim side of me, like most religious fanatics, is all they care about. And what about the guy Lena slept with? I'm sure he's a hero among his guy friends, and these gossiping bitches who are acting like I did something and looking at me like I'm a whore have nothing to say about him. FUCK ALL OF YOU!"

Miriam screamed and stomped her foot.

"Sister, stop that"

The group turned to Salim who opened his arms allowing Miriam to rush into them. She held him shaking and people stopped and gawked.

"I'll walk her to your dorm Orchid".

Orchid twirled the hair on her forearm.

"That's not a good idea Salim. You'll make it worse. People are already staring at you two embracing. I know you care and she's your friend, but don't make life hard for her".

Salim's neck muscles contracted.

"She's not my friend, she's my sister. So you walk with us to show your support."

The director extinguished his pipe and emptied the contents on the ground.

"If she doesn't, I will. Wagging tongues have never bothered me. I married a Christian and they tried to shame me but failed/Let's go Salim. Are you two walking with us?"

The five linked arms and strode across the campus. Midway to the women's dorm, Yusuf joined them and they laughed together until they reached the women's dorm.

The professor refilled his pipe.

"Why don't you all join me for dinner this evening? Say in two hours? I'm a good cook and I'd love to share my record collection with you. There's one thing the Russians imparted while they were here. A love of good music and especially Jazz. My place is easy to find because my house is painted blue. I'm sure you've heard about it".

The professor, Salim and Yusuf turned leaving the women outside the dorm. Miriam straightened her back and taking out a pick, fluffed her hair.

"Well let's get it on. I appreciate you two having my back but it's not necessary. I'm a Muslim and a Jew so I'm accustomed to battling with people to maintain my dignity. I guess I didn't expect it here. Silly me".

Shahknoza linked her arm into Miriam's.

"If having your back means supporting you and being your friend you don't have to thank me. I know how it feels to have people treat you as if something's wrong with you".

Orchid took Miriam's other arm.

"Let's go".

The three women entered the dorm and the conversations in the hallway of young women ceased. Some women snickered. The three women walked through the center of the groups with their heads up, eyes straight ahead, ascended the steps and stopped outside Orchid's door, seeing the word whore written on it. Shahknoza's door had the same word scribbled on it. Shahknoza turned and ran down the steps to the full hallway.

'Whoever wrote this on our doors step out right now and say it to my face so that I can beat you to the ground. Come on. Oh you're cowards. You can write something behind our backs but you're not brave enough to say it to my face. Oh. I'll give you one minute and anyone standing in the hall I'm going to beat you to the ground, rip your clothes off and drag you outside naked for everyone to see you".

The girls in the dorm scattered, running to their rooms and Shahknoza threw her head back bellowing a full stomach laugh. She then walked into the kitchen area and taking a bottle of Windex walked up the stairs, washed the word off her and Orchid's door, then returned the bottle to the kitchen and walking backwards ascended the stairs again.

"You can come out now cowards. We're going into our rooms. But let me tell you something. If you even look at us cross eyed, our say something, I'm going to do what I said".

Going inside Orchid's room, they heard doors opening and voices as they sat on Orchid's bed. Miriam embraced Shahknoza.

"You're crazier than I am".

Shahknoza rubbed her thick toes.

"I'm not crazy. My people changed the face of this land and we have no fear. We're fierce warriors and they know it. My only question is what will you do when we're not with you Miriam?"

Miriam stood and did a series of martial arts moves and kicks.

"I'll defend myself if I have to but there's something I've learned about people. If you let them know you don't care what they think and that they can't control you, they'll leave you alone".

Orchid and Shahknoza agreed.

The three women chatted about school, the Uzbek women telling Miriam about the medical department, then dozed a bit, showered, and readied themselves for the dinner with the Professor.

Walking into the professor's house, Miriam, Shahknoza, Orchid, Yusuf and Salim removed their shoes, slipped on the house slippers the professor

provided, then scanned the professor's living room

with bucked eyes. Stepping down into the sunken

floor, they rubber necked looking at the purple and

gold cloth hanging from the ceiling with bells which

rang with each person passing, bird's which chirped

and sang from corners in the rooms, paintings of

ancient Uzbek warriors, high chairs covered with

gold and purple cloth, and a seven pronged pipe

sitting in the middle of the floor. The dining room

had a flat three-foot table in the floor's middle,

sitting on a fur rug and surrounded by cushions. The

outer walls also had rectangular cushions which sat

against it and had floor cushions with arm rests half

the height of the back rests. The music room was

huge, with a baby grand piano, a western drum set,

bass, with percussion, wind and brass instruments

from every part of the world. The group passed by a

door which the doctor paused before, then opened it. The smell and smoke of sandalwood incense hung in the air and the doctor opened his mouth and using both hands with closed eyes finger motioned the smoke into his mouth. The room only had a black thick rug on the floor. Orchid stepped into the room and her feet sank and were covered by the rug.

"It smells like her in here".

Shahknoza joined her and inhaled.

"Yes it does. Whenever she walked into a room we smelled sandalwood".

The doctor ushered them out of the room.

"I keep an incense burning. Have you noticed though you don't smell it anywhere else? That was her room and I think she inhabits it".

Shahknoza jumped from the room. Passing the master bedroom, they went into a spacious kitchen which opened onto walled in patio. The backyard was covered in flowers. Miriam stopped at the back door.

"Your garden's all overgrown. You haven't pruned it in a long time".

The doctor wiped his forehead.

"I have no idea what to do. Strangely, none of the plants have died in five years. I just let it grow. You're welcome to show me what to do, though the weather will be changing soon".

Miriam patted her cheeks.

'I'd love to. My mother had a garden and my fondest memories are working in it with her".

Shahknoza opened the back door.

"Working together is something new couples should do together because it builds your union. When Yusuf and I get married I want to have a flower garden with plants that will grow year around. There are about five of them out there".

The group turned to her and Orchid popped her friend on the bottom.

'You know about plants Shahknoz? I had no idea".

Yusuf fluffed Shahknoza's hair.

"Her grandmother used to sell them in the market in our hometown though the Russians tried to stop her. Behind her house was a hill of medicinal plants. She cured many people. That's where Shahknoz got her love of biology from and why she likes research".

Orchid kissed her friend's cheek.

"My father always says you never know someone".

The doctor turned off the backyard light.

"You never do and that's why friendships, like life, are interesting and full of surprises".

They stood in the kitchen talking and drinking, the men, Shahknoz and Miriam drinking wine and Orchid juice until the food was warmed and each made their plates then sat on the floor at the dining room table and enjoyed themselves sharing childhood stories. They played music after the meal and the evening was topped off with Orchid and Shahknoza dancing to the group playing percussion instruments. Putting on their jackets because a brisk wind whistled through the campus, Shahknoza elbowed Orchid when the doctor reached for Miriam's hand.

"Would you help me clean my dishes".

Miriam made circles with her thumbs on each pinky.

"I would if I didn't have to get up early for a class. You can make me dinner another time and I'll not only clean, I'll cook and if you like, tuck you in".

The professor rubbed his earlobe.

"I haven't been tucked in since my mother used to bathe me then powder me all over. Will that be included?"

Miriam batted her eyes.

"One never knows, does one? Let's go ladies, it's getting late".

Taking Orchid and Salim's arms, she pulled them from the door, leaving the professor standing there. She breathed through her nose.

"Orchid, is he still standing there?"
Orchid glanced over her shoulder,
"Yes he is, and the light's still on. Are you going back Miriam?"

Miriam exhaled.

"I want to, but I won't. Men like mystery and having something too soon spoils the hunt. Isn't that true Salim?"

Salim nodded, then turning waved his hand at the doctor, and squeezed Miriam's hand.

"He just turned off the light and closed the door" Miriam looked back.

"I'm glad you two are walking with me. My knees are weak".

Orchid searched for Miriam's eyes in the darkness, then turned to watch Shahknoza and Yusuf strolling together, swinging their arms. Her heart swung with each step, her stomach moved like a snake on the ground and she took deep breaths, inhaling Salim's cologne. Miriam sang *Love Is In The Air*, snapping her fingers in a disco beat and they quickened their pace matching Miriam's snapping. The three stopped in front of the women's dorm and Miriam released Orchid and Salim's arms and entered the building. She pointed her finger at Salim, but stopped when he followed Orchid's head facing Miriam. Orchid, wiped dripping palms on her jacket, and gave Salim a bent arm.

"Thank you for accompanying me. I had a wonderful time"

Yusuf removed his tinted glasses.

"As did I and I hope we'll spend more evenings together. I hear you're a runner?"

Orchid tried to drop Salim's hand but he held it, rubbing his fingers over her knuckles. Orchid's thighs twitched.

"Yes I am. Yusuf told you"

Salim touched the perspiration on her palm.

"Athletes always talk about other athletes. You're one of the best in your country"

Orchid removed her tingling hand and placed both hands between her legs.

"I used to be. I haven't trained in years, but I still love to run".

"Then I'll meet you at five thirty in the morning and we'll run the hills"

Orchid moved forward with a push from Shahknoza behind her.

"I'll see you then. Good night".

She turned and weak jellied legs struggled to the doorway and entered. Miriam raised her eyebrows.

"Don't turn around because he's still standing there. He's taken off his glasses and is wiping his eyes. I think he's crying. Oh Orchid, he's in love with you. I've known him all my life and I've never seen him emotional about anyone. Okay, he turned and he's running. If you turn around quickly you can see him".

Orchid spun around and caught a glimpse of Salim's long strides gliding under the lamplight and into the cloak of night.

The three women ascended the stairs and entered Orchid's room. Shahknoza sat next to Orchid, cradled her head and kissed her on the forehead.

"I know it's difficult for you Miss control. Sometimes you just have to let go Orchid. This is love at first sight and both of you feel it. Remember in biology? It's called pheromones".

Orchid lifted her head.

"I know Shahknoz. Miriam, why didn't you stay with the professor? You two have love at first sight too".

Miriam removed her clothes, bra, and wearing only her panties sat on the other bed assigned to her. The two Uzbek women giggled and exchanged a look. Miriam saw it.

"An Uzbek girl wouldn't be walking around like this would she?"

Orchid and Shahknoza's downward looks answered her.

"Not in front of a stranger. Maybe a sister, but not someone not a family member. They'd even be shy in front of their husbands"

Miriam studied her palms.

"I gave you one reason before and you just gave another reason. He's not accustomed to a western woman's freedom and he'd probably think less of me for making love with him on the first date".

Shahknoza stood and removed her dress and bra.

"I'm not sure, but I don't think the professor's like that. You never know though with men. They have two faces. One for them and one for us".

The three women slapped fives. Orchid removed her socks and the other two women chuckled, making Orchid throw her hands into the air and twist her bottom. Shahknoza and Miriam wrestled Orchid to the floor and pulled off her pants. Orchid removed her blouse, bra and threw them in Shahknoza's face.

"Are you happy now?"
Shahknoza turned her back to Orchid and mooned her.

"I'll be happy when you remove those panties"
Orchid gave her the finger and focused on Miriam.

"Miriam, how could you have known Salim all his life? We heard him say you were his

sister but we thought he meant something else".

Miriam reached for her purse.

"He's my brother. My real brother".

Orchid and Shahknoza's movements stalled.

"How can he be your brother? His skin's a different color".

Orchid took a picture Miriam held out to them.

"And he has a different last name".

She and Shahknoza stared at the picture Miriam had handed them. Orchid gasped.

"There are five different kinds of people all together in this family and the older people are also different. One looks Asian and the other is black, like Salim. Why?"

Miriam took the picture.

"This is our family and these are my siblings. These are our parents. Not our blood parents, but the only parents we know. They're our foster parents. That's our brother Khaled, his original parents were from

Korea and the U.S, Muhammad's parents were from Egypt and the U.S., Khalema's parents were from Scotland and the U.S., there's Salim, his parents were both from the U.S. and then there's me, my parents were from Israel and Morocco, but we were all raised from babies together. So this is my family and we're all almost doctors".

Headlights showed in the two women's faces.

Orchid blinked and closed her mouth.

"And you're all Muslims".

Miriam kissed the picture and placed it in her bag.

"We were born Muslims and know all our prayers and stuff. None of us practice and our parents aren't strict at all".

Shahknoza wagged her finger.

"Like mine and most people here except for those Koran wavers who do everything everyone does except they hide it and condemn everyone else".

Orchid's hands flew to her hips.

"Shahknoz"

Shahknoza sat cross legged on the floor.

"Sorry Orchid, I know your family's religious and not like that, but most people are and you know it".

Orchid sucked her lip and joined Shahknoza and now Miriam on the floor. Orchid reached for Miriam's hands.

"I dreamed about falling in love like this and now I have it with your brother. This is like becoming part of a family".

Miriam grasped Orchid and Shahknoza's hands.

"Yes it is and you two are sisters".

CHAPTER TWO

Orchid ran in place after stretching and adjusted her ankle braces by tightening the Velcro which secured them. Hearing laughter and footsteps, she raised her head and watched as the soccer team passed her without giving her a nod, followed by Yusuf and Salim, their teeth showing with smiles. Orchid joined them and quickened her pace. Yusuf raised his hand.

"Whoa, we're not running with them, we're going to my car and the Chimgan mountains".

Orchid slowed her pace, Salim ran backwards and they trotted to Yusuf's car where Shahknoza bent and stretched.

"Are you ready Orchid. The mountain awaits us. It's much better than running through the campus and around the track".

Orchid surveyed Yusuf's new Audi.

"Where'd you get this car?"

Yusuf polished the door with his elbow.

"It was a gift from the government".

Shahknoza rubbed her bottom against the hood.

"And it's all ours. We have the registration. Get in Orchid and enliven it with your fragrance".

Orchid and Shahknoza sat in the back seat and Shahknoza jabbered the entire one and a half-hour drive. Arriving at the Chimgan mountain, they exited and stretched again. Yusuf bent his knees and pointed to the left side of the mountain.

"We're going to run this way, it's more scenic".

Orchid angled her head to the right.

"Let's go Salim, this way it's a better run".

Orchid waved to Yusuf and Shahknoza, and began at a quick pace with Salim matching her stride for stride. They circled the first level of the mountain then began to climb. Orchid loved the swoosh of the air blowing past her ears and the air which filled her lungs and made her eyes widen. Climbing the hill, they passed a few fires in the darkness with people cooking. She felt Salim's shoulders brush hers and wondered if he'd be able to stay with her as they jogged higher and higher in the darkness with the daylight easing its way into the air. Three fourths up the mountain four hunters with rifles and gear carrying a dead leopard on a pole tried to halt them.

"We've seen other big cats tracks higher up so you'd better not go to high. They're mating and in hunting season. Be careful".

Orchid waved them off and continued running, pumping her arms for more speed and power.

Glancing at Salim she noticed he barely breathed and smiled at her.

"I like this pace and running up the mountain. I used to train by running the hills in California".

Orchid focused on the trail.

"So you're used to running upward"

Salim raised his thumbs.

"It's the best way to train for any sport".

They turned a bend and jumped over a long metal pole and stopped as four bear cubs ran in front of them. Salim grabbed Orchid.

"Stop. The mother must be near."

The bear's roar interrupted his sentence and the mother bear, saliva dripping from its mouth paused long enough for Salim to push Orchid behind him. She fell to the ground and scooted backwards, her heart in her throat. Salim glanced back at her and bent down twisted the metal pole as the bear

charged. Orchid covered her face.

"Salim!"

They heard barking and a Chihuahua darted past

them towards the bear, being chased by the cubs.

The mother bear raised on its hind legs and Salim

grabbed the pole and grunting threw it at the bear.

The pole went through the bear's chest, blood

squirted from its mouth along with a gurgling sound

and it side stepped and fell backwards, the pole

lodging in the ground. Orchid leapt from the ground

onto Salim's back, wrapping her arms around his

neck, and kissed him on the head, neck, ears, cheek

and neck. His breath came in staccato bursts, his

body a block of muscle and he gawked at the dead

bear until a voice called the Chihuahua which

dodged the cubs ambling towards their dead mother.

Orchid and Salim turned to see a hunter in army

fatigues lifting the dog, kissing it and placing it in his pocket after placing a small muzzle on it. Shahknoza hurried to Orchid and tried to pry Orchid's arms from around Salim's neck. Orchid kicked at Shahknoza.

"No, no, no Shahknoz, I almost lost him. No, no, no".

The hunter fired his gun into the air three times, then he and Yusuf began to clap. They were soon joined by four other hunters, all carrying rifles, who strode to the dead bear, then turned and clapped for Salim who still hadn't moved. Salim carried Orchid to the bear and looked down at the gigantic dead animal. One hunter lifted a huge paw.

"She's the biggest one I've ever seen. Look at how big her cubs are".

The cubs sat around their mother's head, whimpering. The same hunter removed his knife, sliced off the claws from one of the bear's paws, placed them in a plastic baggy and handed it to Salim, who took the baggy and pressed it to his chest. He lowered Orchid to the ground and she released his neck, then looked down at herself. She'd wet herself. Shahknoza walked Orchid away from the men and they headed down the mountain, followed by Yusuf and Salim, whose body shook.

Shahknoza pulled Orchid into a run and they scampered down the mountain. Reaching the bottom, Shahknoza opened the Audi's trunk and grabbing some clothes, a towel and a bottle of water pushed Orchid to the back door and opening it dragged her inside the car.

"Take off those wet pants Orchid and wash."

Orchid sat with her eyes open, staring straight ahead. Shahknoza removed Orchid's pants, washed her, put on the clean sweat pants and rolling the wet one's into a ball, open the car and put them in the trunk. A vendor selling ice drinks with sweet flavoring stood a few feet from the car so Shahknoza bought five cones of ice and opening the car door, poured the ice into Orchid's top and rubbed her face with the rest. Orchid shook her head and raising, bumped her head against the car's interior roof.

"Shahknoz. What are you doing?"

She rolled from the car and stood, shaking the ice from her top.

"That's cold Shahknoz"

Shahknoza rubbed a bit more ice on Orchid's face.

"I had to wake you up Orchid. You were in a little bit of shock. Do you remember anything?"

Orchid pushed Shahknoza's hand away.

"Of course I do. We almost got killed by a bear and Salim saved us. I'm blank after that".

Shahknoza guided Orchid to the trunk and opening it, spread out the pants, then lifting them put them to Orchid's face.

"You did that and I changed you".

Orchid slapped the wet pants from Shahknoza's hand and slammed the trunk shut.

"Oh my God. I don't remember. Did anyone see you"

Shahknoza watched Yusuf and Salim reach the mountain's last plateau.

"No, no one saw you. Now let's drink some warm camel milk". They sipped the warm milk as Yusuf and Salim reached the bottom of the mountain. Yusuf motioned for the two women to get into the car. They all entered and Salim sat in the front seat and immediately fell asleep. Yusuf watched Orchid opening and closing her hands in his rear view mirror, and spoke to Shahknoza in their village dialect he knew Orchid didn't understand.

"is she alright?"

Shahknoza blinked both eyes.

"I think she'll be fine once she rests. That bear wouldn't have had to attack me because I'd have died on the spot"

Yusuf drummed the steering wheel.

"Thank God for the hunter and that Fice. It saved them. Look, she's gone".

Orchid had slumped against the window and was asleep. Shahknoza placed a jacket over sister/friend.

"I'd sleep too if I came that close to death."

Shahknoza and Yusuf watched their two friends sleep until they reached the campus. Salim sat up in the passenger's seat.

"Yusuf, did that really happen or was I dreaming?"
Yusuf raised his hand for a high five.
"it really happened. You killed a mammoth sized bear with basically a spear. Its claws are in your lap".

Salim raised the plastic bag and examined its contents.
"Damn. We could have been killed".
Yusuf fist pumped Salim's shoulder.
"That you could have but you didn't and you saved your and Orchid's life".
Salim moved his body to see Orchid who still slept.
"Damn, damn, damn. That was close".

Reaching the campus and parking the car, Orchid watched as it took Salim three attempts to exit the car.

"Yusuf, man, my legs feel like jelly. Would you mind helping me up?"

Yusuf helped Salim to his feet and supported him with his first few steps.

"Are you okay brother?"

Salim removed his arm from around Yusuf's neck.

"Yes, I got it now"

He took easy light steps, then, shaking his head, walked with his normal long strides. Orchid marveled at his soccer round butt muscles showing through his light blue jogging pants. She noted to herself that he liked blue, and wanted to see him in a light blue shirt. A thump on the head snapped her back to reality.

"Stop that".

Shahknoza stood wide legged, her hands spread and gripping her hips. Orchid thumped her back.

"What?"

Shahknoza flicked her head at Salim.

"You're staring at his ass".

Orchid covered her mouth and looped her arm in Shahknoza's.

"I think I'm still not right yet. I've never been so scared in my life. Shahknoz, I could smell her rage. She was going to kill us".

Chanting attracted their attention and they turned to see what it was. A group of students chanted "qirivchi" as Salim passed them. Salim spun and watched them as they passed.

"What does that mean?"

Yusuf held his head.

"It mean's bear killer. I don't know how, but the word has already gotten around".

The name calling continued as they crossed the campus and separated, going to their dorms.

....

8 hours later, Orchid and Shahknoza noticed Miriam and Salim walking across campus in their white doctor's coats. Miriam had her arm around Salim's waist, his arm rested on her shoulders, and they laughed throwing their heads back at some joke shared between them. Salim nodded to people who spoke to him as he passed, and he and Miriam laughed more after each person spoke. Orchid quickened her step.

"Look at how they walk Shahknoz. They're very proud and confident. I never noticed but she's almost as tall as he is."

Shahknoza squeezed Orchid's arm.

"You're not looking at her."

They followed the two Americans across the campus to the little café where they'd last seen and spoken to Siroj. Dr. Ziyod stood outside the café smoking his pipe. Seeing Salim and Miriam, he poured the tobacco from his pipe and embraced both. Orchid and Shahknoza reached them as the hug ended and they all greeted each other. Salim, eyes melting, looked down at Orchid.

"Are you okay? I've had a few shaky moments throughout the day".
Orchid made a muscle.
"I'm fine, thanks to you".
Salim pointed upward.
"Thanks be to something stronger than us, Allah."
Shahknoza cleared her throat.
"Uh oh. Somebody's watching".
The group turned to see Siroj, red faced, watching them from the window inside and surrounded by a

group of men. She waved at them and nudged Orchid.

"Isn't that the boxer who won the European championship and is on his way to America?"

Ziyod clapped his hands.

"Yes, that's him and he probably wants to meet the bear killer" Salim stiffened.

"I wish people wouldn't call me that. I don't think I did anything heroic. It was a desperate act to survive and protect Orchid".

Shahknoza jumped in the air.

"He said it. He said it. He said it Orchid".

Orchid studied her feet trying to hide the color smothering her face. Miriam took Salim's arm.

"Let's go inside and have a drink. I'm told people drink here on the down low".

Orchid pulled Miriam towards her.

"Women aren't allowed inside here. We can go somewhere else"

Miriam said what without words.

"Damn. So it's like that huh?"

Doctor Ziyod refilled his pipe.

"I'm sorry but yes it is."

Miriam took out a rolled cigarette and lit it. The smell of burnt rags filled the air. Salim took the cigarette from Miriam and used his fingers to extinguish the flame.

"Miriam, not here".

Miriam crossed her arms and rocked back on her heels.

"I'm not leaving. Buy me a drink and I'll drink it right here".

The doctor removed his pipe.

"She's not moving Doctor. I know my sister. We'll have to do as she says or she'll make a scene. Miri, you're crazy. Let's buy her a drink and come outside Doc".

The doctor opened the door and Salim followed him. Siroj stood in the doorway.

"You can come inside doctor but he can't".

The professor froze.

"What do you mean he can't? This club belongs to the university. Now move".

Siroj crossed his arms and the tall bearded boxer with the beaked nose sneered, showing all his teeth.

"It's on university land but this is a private club and we say who comes in. You can come in but he can't".

Shahknoza spit on the ground in front of Siroj. The doctor turned and guided Salim with a hand on Salim's shoulder.

"This place is beneath you Salim. Let's go somewhere else that doesn't smell bad".

Salim gave Siroj and the others a closed mouth smile and turned to go. The bearded fighter cracked his knuckles.

"He's from America so he's used to being denied entrance into places".

Fist balled Salim spun around.

"What the fuck is that supposed to mean muthafucka?"

Miriam threw down her bag.

"Yea, what are you trying to say motherfucka?"

The boxer stepped from the club along with Siroj and the other men inside the club.

"You know what I'm mean. You, black people are second class citizens so you're accustomed to not being allowed to enter places. And we're treating you the same here because of what you are. They have a name for you beginning with a "N", and I don't have to use it because you know what I mean".

The doctor locked his hands around Salim and held him.

"Let's go Salim. He's not worth it. He's trying to provoke you but don't let him".

Salim snapped his neck from side to side.

"Let me go doctor. He's looking for a fight, and he's got one".

The boxer cracked his knuckles again.

"Yes. Let him go. Muhammad Ali is an old punch drunk fighter and probably the father he doesn't know. Bear killer"

Miriam kicked off her shoes.

"You're saying something about my family".

Shahknoza and Orchid held Miriam whose face contorted.

'Kick his ass Salim".

The doctor released Salim and moved to the side. The fighter, seeing an opening stepped forward with his hands up and threw a left jab. Salim leaned backwards away from the punch and spun landing a roundhouse back kick to the fighter's temple. The fighter's legs stiffened, his head jerked back with the whites showing in both eyes and both knees buckled. Salim ran forward snapping the fighter's head backwards with left jabs then stepped forward and grunted as he threw an uppercut. The boxer's body fell backwards knocking the door off its hinges and with glass breaking he landed on top of the door, spread eagled with his legs twitching. Salim grabbed a trash can and lifted it above his head. Orchid and Shahknoza screamed and let go of

Miriam who ran past Salim, now held by the doctor and kicked the unconscious boxer between the legs three times. Siroj tried to push her but she moved around his arms and kicked him in the testicles twice. He doubled over and crumpled to the ground writhing. Miriam stared down at him as she hit him upside the head with an elbow, then assisted the doctor in easing Salim's arms down with the trash can. Salim lowered the can then poured the trash over Siroj, the unconscious fighter and tossed the can. He and Miriam walked backwards from the building watching the men standing outside. Miriam brandished her middle finger.

"The next time watch who you're fucking with and who you're calling a Nigger. You muthafukas".

The doctor, his head swinging like a pendulum walked with Orchid and Shahknoza.

"I'm very ashamed that they'd treat Salim like that.
I would have never imagined something like this
could happen here. I'll make sure that young man is
gone from the university today".

Salim stopped walking backwards.

"Don't do that doctor. This was between me and
them and has nothing to do with the school. They
have a right to have anyone they want in their club
and I don't have a problem with that. Plus, what
happened wasn't about what it seemed. It was about
something else. Or should I say someone else".

He focused on Orchid, then taking Miriam's hand
they left Orchid, Shahknoza and Ziyod. Orchid
watched the brother and sister striding across the
campus with their heads in the air.

"He's right doctor. It was about something else. Please don't report Siroj. Being expelled will ruin his life."

The doctor contemplated his pipe then excused himself leaving the two women alone.

Orchid pulled her coat tighter and blew into her palms.

'Men are so violent Shahknoz"

Shahknoza threw a few punches.

"They are, and I enjoyed watching that half Russian be knocked out. I like boxing".

Arm in arm they moved across the campus feeling the darkness approaching. Orchid heard her name called and turned towards the voice. A medium small shouldered height woman with an oval shaped face, crater sized eyes, big breasts and thin but firm legs wearing a tan dress and shoes to match waved at her. Orchid waved and approached the woman with short steps.

"Auntie. I didn't know you're on campus today".

They kissed on both cheeks and the woman took Orchid's arm as they approached Shahknoza, who bowed her head and kissed the woman on both cheeks.

"Good evening doctor!"

Orchid's aunt sucked her teeth.

"How long have I known you Shahknoza?"

"Maybe fifteen years Ms."

"And you're still calling me doctor? I told you a long time ago to call me auntie. How's Yusuf?"

"He's fine auntie. He's training very hard and anxious to finish here".

The doctor opened her tan purse, pulled out an envelope and handed it to Shahknoza.

"Here give this to him, but I'll tell you first. I reevaluated all his credits and those courses he took in America have been counted. He has enough units to graduate and doesn't have to come study the next semester. Technically he's finished everything here so he can play professionally if he wants".

Shahknoza held the envelope to her breast and running yelled over her shoulder.

"Orchid I'll see you in a little while. I have to tell Yusuf now."

The two women laughed watching Shahknoza's hair streaming back as she waved the envelope in the air. Orchid's aunt moved her in another direction.

"I heard you had a close call with a bear".

Orchid felt perspiration gathering at the base of her skull.

"I did auntie and it was terrifying. If"

Her aunt angled her head at Orchid.

"If it weren't for qirivchi you'd be dead".

"His name is Salim auntie".

Orchid's aunt pulled her closer.

"I know his name and you know I do. He's the most brilliant young surgeon I've ever taught and he has the most skill full and delicate hands I've ever seen. It's as if they're magic. His sister's the same. They're special people".

Orchid looked upward, but her aunt stopped and pulled Orchid's face downward.

"And you love him".

Orchid reached in her pocket for a tissue but her aunt gave her a handkerchief.

"People are whispering Orchid and it's gotten to me, so I'm sure it's reached your father".

Lead lodged in Orchid's feet and she bent her knees to lift them.

"What should I do auntie? You know my father".

Auntie rubbed shoulders with Orchid as they walked.

"What you always do when confronted with any obstacle. Be proactive. Now come with me to my clinic. I want you to see something. Still not squeamish about blood?" Orchid bumped her aunt with her hip.

"You know I'm not auntie."

Her aunt bumped her back.

'I still think you're missing your calling by going into diplomacy. You should have been a doctor like me".

Shoulders touching, they walked across the campus and entered the clinic with the full emergency room smelling of tobacco, snuff, sweat, and full of shrivel faced men wearing cofis and scarf headed toothless men and women from the countryside. Auntie led Orchid through the emergency room and into a hallway with antiseptic resting in the air.

"Remove your jacket and come with me. I need to scrub and you need to be sanitized".

Orchid followed her aunt into a room where she changed into white socks, special cloth shoes, a head covering, mask and gloves. Her aunt went into another room, scrubbed her hands, arms, then waited while an assistant eased her gloves over her hands, down her arms and walked with her into an operating room. Orchid followed her aunt and stood around the operating table. Salim stood over a patient next to Miriam and they both wore a visor with a light in the front. Auntie took her position between he and Miriam.

"Salim, begin the operation."

Orchid watched Salim make an incision, part the patient's skin after a clamp had been applied and begin slicing and removing something from the patient. She watched her aunt's eyes smile and her ears move back showing she was pleased. Auntie sucked in her breath.

"Miriam, would you take over now?"
Miriam continued Salim's work until Auntie nodded.
"Salim close".
Salim pulled the open wound together with his right hand and sewed the sutures with his left hand. Auntie's mask expanded with her breath.

"Well, we're finished here. Excellent job you two. Excellent. I'll see you in the next room."

Lifting her head, auntie gave Orchid the signal to leave, and Orchid went into the scrubbing room.

Her aunt entered and moving her head allowed her mask to drop.

"Did you see them? Amazing! We have one more surgery to do and then we'll be free. Do you want to see mama?"

Orchid replaced her auntie's mask.

"I'd like to, Auntie, but I have a major exam tomorrow and I want to refresh my notes. I'll see her on the weekend. Bye Auntie".

Her aunt's mouth moved as if sending a kiss and she disappeared through swinging doors. Orchid changed her clothes and strutted into the night air. Walking, she sang a song she'd heard Salim play on his portable disk recorder. He said it was one of his mother's favorites.

May I have a word with you?

I'd like to tell you yeah

What I've been going through

My nights are so long

As I watch each hour go by

Hoping and praying yeah

That Some day I'll be your guy

Hey Love

You're my one true soul desire

Hey love, baby

Can you feel this burning desire

Hey love

There's one thing I find so true

When you are near me

I go through a change or two

Hearing your footsteps

I hurry to catch your eye

I stand there waiting, yeah

But girl you just walk on by

Say love

With a cold heart you are dealing

Hey love, yeah

It's an awful hurting feeling

Hey love

Don't pass me without some sign

Just look me over yeah

You might want to change your mind.

She sang and bounced on the balms of her feet
doing what he said his parents had called the
Temptations Walk, not caring who saw her or the
people staring as she sang and moved to the songs
floating from within her. And she knew, at that
moment, he was her heart, the stream which flowed
in every direction within her, and others eyes and
ears were non-existent. Twirling and dancing, she
sang My Cherie Amour, All I do and skipped across
the campus shouting September by Earth Wind and
Fire. Arriving at her dorm she threw kisses into the

air, bowed to the world and screamed in English

Kiss my ass if you don't appreciate him and went

inside taking the steps two at a time. Knocking on

Shahknoza's door her friend opened it and Orchid

lifted her and swung her around. Shahknoza moved

away from Orchid.

"What's got into you? You're never like this"
Orchid disrobed and strutted around her friend's

room naked.

"I saw him Shahknoz. Today I saw him. Before I

saw him save my life, and fight for me, and today

operate on someone. Shahknoz, he glowed with

confidence and pride and brilliance and ease and I

love him and I don't care who knows and we will

have beautiful tall brown babies with curly wild hair

and I feel them and him down here Shaknoz. Down

here".

Orchid held her hands between her legs and opened them as if she were throwing what lived there into the air. Shaknoz sat on her bed watching her friend and waited until she spread herself flat on the floor doing pushups. Shahknoz tossed a sheet of paper to her.

"There's one more way you'll have to see him tonight and it may not be pretty".

Orchid jackknifed upward and read the sheet of paper. Salim had been challenged to a fight at the gym by the best martial artist in Tashkent who wanted to restore his brother, the knocked out boxer's honor. Chill bumps rose all over Orchid's body and she covered herself to fend off the cold.

"He can't challenge him. Salim's a doctor not a fighter. He might hurt his hands or get beat up. The half Russian's a professional and he fights for a living. It won't be fair".

"it won't be fair for the other guy and you don't have to worry about my brother. I just hope he contains himself and doesn't kill the guy."

Miriam had walked through the door and stood open legged with an unlit hand rolled cigarette in her mouth. Orchid held up the paper.

"You know about this?"

Miriam closed the door and sat on Shahknoza's bed.

"Of course. They came to the clinic and gave it to him personally. If you're going you'd better come now because I'm sure it'll be packed".

Orchid hurried into her clothes as they descended the steps and almost trotted to the gymnasium. Orchid tugged at Miriam's jacket.

"Do you think Salim will get hurt?"

Miriam laughed until she had to clear her throat.

"He's a six-degree black belt and he started boxing when he was three. Plus, he knows five different forms of Martial arts. My only concern is how long he'll let it last and if he wants to punish the guy. If this guy's brother uses the "n" word, it will be bloody".

The gymnasium was full and dense with cigarette smoke. The three women entered and moved through the crowd to where Salim and Yusuf sat. Salim held his toes and wiggled his body. Orchid sat next to him and opened her hand, but Miriam grabbed it.

"Don't touch him and don't talk to him. He needs to focus. If you see a red line appear on the side of his face, move away".

Shahknoza held onto Yusuf who sat her in a chair behind him. He watched the ring, he bobbed his head as Dr. Ziyod and Orchid's auntie entered the gym. Auntie carried her doctor's bag and Ziyod chewed his pipe's stem. Auntie stood behind Salim who still hadn't looked up. The crowd cheered as the Uzbek Russian climbed into the ring. His purple faced and eyed boxer brother held an Uzbek flag which he waved, then pulled out an American flag and threw it on the floor. The crowd stopped cheering. The brother then unfolded a red, green and black flag and set it on fire. The crowd remained silent while the brothers laughed. Smelling the fire, Salim looked up, his muscles rippled and the red line appeared on his cheek. Miriam stepped back. Auntie coughed.

"Do you see how people are here Miriam. A personal fight is between two men. But when they made it about someone's country and their culture, they wouldn't go for it. These Uzbek Russians have gone too far. Hurt him Salim".

Salim shimmied and walked barefoot to the ring and up the stairs. An older man wearing white Martial Arts gear bowed to both fighter's and stepped away. The Uzbek Russian circled, faked a kick and advanced punching and kicking. Salim used his knees, forearms, feet and shoulders to block the punches, then threw a straight closed fist punch to the other fighter's forehead, which snapped the fighter's head back, then an elbow to the nose which spewed blood. Another blow turned the fighter's head sideways towards his brother and blood splattered across the first rows, soaking people's faces. Salim sent a right kick to the inner thigh, four right and left hand punches to the solar plexus bending him over, open hand fist punches to the chin, a knee to the solar plexus, forearm to the chin, straightening him up, elbows to the head sending him sideways, then he grabbed his arm by the wrist, pushing at the center of the arm which made a snapping sound, as the crowd groaned, and finally a right hook knocking him on his back, blood bubbling from his mouth. Salim pivoted on his right foot and left the ring, steering clear of everyone. Getting to the gym door he kicked it open and growling walked into the night. Auntie climbed into the ring and began attending to the unconscious fighter. Orchid, Shahknoza and the doctor focused on Miriam.

"Leave him alone. He'll come around when he's ready. He's always hated violence".

Auntie called Ziyod's name and motioned for him to call an ambulance. He ran to the gymnasium office and auntie then beckoned to Miriam, who joined her along with Orchid in the ring and squatted next to the fighter.

"I need your help. He has internal bleeding, I think his liver's been perforated and most of the bones in his face have been crushed so he'll need reconstructive surgery. Can you do it?"

Miriam looked at the broken fighter with blood coming from his ears, nose and mouth.

"Of course, a doctor treats everyone."

Ziyod, the fighter's brother and two other men lifted the fighter onto a stretcher and carried him to the ambulance. Orchid rode with them to the clinic, focusing on the brother who held his brother's hand and urged his brother to hold on and fight for his life. The ambulance stopped in front of the clinic and exiting the ambulance auntie paused.

"The lights are on inside."

The door opened and Salim, dressed in green scrubs ran from the clinic pushing a gurney.

"We better hurry. That last punch ruptured his spleen."

They ran with the gurney pushing it into the clinic. The fighter's brother pulled Salim's top before he entered the operating room.

"Thank you for helping my brother and I'm sorry for what I said. If I hadn't said that he wouldn't be in this situation. Siroj told me to say that".

Salim walked backwards to the operating room.

"It's all good but he didn't force you to say what you did. Don't give it a second thought."

The doors closed leaving the brother watching the door. Orchid approached the brother and joined him as he deposited his massive frame into a chair.

"Don't worry about your brother, he's in good hands".

His head dropped into both hands.

"I should have never let him fight. I knew he couldn't beat that champion. He's too skilled and powerful. Pride is foolish. If he dies, I'll never forgive myself".

Orchid was distracted by the front door opening. Siroj, his head dragging, entered the clinic and stood over Orchid and the brother.

"I'm sorry Gustav. It's all my fault. Is Yakov going to be alright?"

The brother raised his shoulders and wept into his hands. Siroj sat next to him and placed an arm around his friend's shoulders. Siroj placed his bottom teeth on his top lip.

"Orchid, I love you and I'm sorry I've been behaving like a child. Jealousy has gotten the best of me. Salim is a good, wonderful man and I hope you two can be happy. Tongues are wagging and

I'm responsible for that too. I'm ashamed and embarrassed. We were friends before and I'd like to be friends again. Could you find it in your heart to forgive me?"

Bile streamed into Orchid's throat, mouth, and tasting the acidic bitterness she swallowed hard, feeling it swirl in her stomach and finally lodge in her bowels, which she clamped.

"I'll try. Trying to hurt Salim wouldn't lead me towards you Siroj. It only makes me hate you".

Siroj looked into his hands.

'I hate myself at this moment".

Orchid gave him an open palm.

"Only God can forgive, and I can't forget, but I can move on from this Siroj. We've known each other too long to let something like this come between us".

They shook hands and sat on each side of Gustav.

Four hours later, Auntie, Miriam and Salim emerged smiling from the operating room. Auntie shook the sleeping Gustav which awakened Orchid and Siroj.

"Your brother's fine. Give him about 30 minutes and you'll be able to talk to him".

Gustav kissed the three doctors' hands.

"Praise God. I thank you from the bottom of my heart".

Auntie narrowed her eyes while looking at Siroj.

"And you're the asshole who started all this. I see you're sitting next to Orchid so she must have forgiven you. Or knowing her she's probably trying to forgive you. Well I don't, and I won't. Never set foot in my clinic again. Now leave".

Mumbling she did an about face and went into her office. Siroj rose to his feet, then dropped to one knee in front of Salim.

"I'm sorry and I ask for your forgiveness".
Salim stepped back, giving Siroj room to stand.
"Don't do that man. You have to forgive yourself because at this moment my heart is full of malice for you and it will take a while for me to get over this. I almost killed that man and you used them to insult me, my country and my people. You walk one way and I'll walk another Siroj, and life will continue. Let me say this to you so that you understand. In my community we have a saying, man up. The next time you have a problem with me, man up, step to me and say it to my face".

Siroj extended his hand for a shake but Salim ignored it and he, along with Miriam, joined auntie in her office.

Siroj opened and closed his hands. Orchid and Gustav observed his hands turn to fists and his shoulders hunched, he left the clinic with heavy steps.

Gustav tapped his feet on the floor.

"I participated in this and I have something in my heart against Siroj, but mainly against myself for allowing myself to be used. I understand qirivchi Salim, but also Siroj. I'm curious though why Siroj was angry. You've known him since you all were children. Do you know why?"

Orchid eyes followed the trail of anger Siroj had left, and she too wondered.

CHAPTER THREE

Orchid lit the fire in Dr. Ziyod's cabin and observed him turn on the heat to warm the chilly cabin in the Chimgan mountains outside Tashkent. She could see the rectangular and square light colored places on the walls where the doctor had removed the pictures she assumed were of he and his wife who'd died in childbirth, along with the child four years ago when she was a freshman at the university. She remembered her as a tall night haired broad shouldered Turkish woman with loose curly hair hanging to the middle of her back, who spoke Uzbek with a Turkish accent and rolled, and smoked her own cigarettes using Turkish tobacco which made the back of Orchid's throat itch. She taught Turkic languages, plus French and English in the diplomat university and had a policy that once a student entered her class, only the language being taught could be spoken. She had liked Orchid, complimenting her on her accent, using her as an example in class of study habits because Orchid was only one of two students, the other being Shahknoza, who checked out and listened to the tapes Mrs. Juraeva had made for the students. Mrs. Juraeva never complimented Shahknoza though because her Tatar accent gave her Turkish and other languages a peculiar sound which Mrs. Juraeva found unpleasant, though she never said it to Shahknoza. Shahknoza listened to the tapes more than Orchid did, and the day before Mrs. Juraeva passed, visited her in the hospital and spoke to her in perfect Turkish, having the same accent as Mrs. Juraeva who finally complemented her. Orchid was present that day and recalled Shahknoza's red nose as she left the hospital, her eyes aflame with pride, but turned downward with sadness. Orchid had comforted her friend with flat hand wide circles on her back.

"Shahknoz, why are you crying so much. You should be happy because she finally complimented you".

Shahknoza had cleared her nose on a handkerchief which she dropped into a trash bin outside the hospital.

"I know that look she has Orchid. My mother had that same look when she died giving birth to my little brother. Do you see how pale her feet were? I could see the veins in them. Pregnant women's feet are healthy. She's going to die Orchid. Believe me. We're going to lose the best professor in our department".

Three hours later Dr. Juraeva was dead at 32, leaving her young husband the doctor alone with his huge record collection which lined the walls of a room they'd built onto their house.

Dr. Juraeva moved close to Orchid.

"I know you're wondering about all my wife's pictures missing from the walls with the imprints still being there. I don't look back Orchid, and to be reminded of her would be looking back. Plus, I've found a new love and I want her to make this place her place. Does that make sense to you?"

Orchid answered with a nod, and feeling the heater and fire's warmth, removed her jacket and walked down the hall to her small room. Removing her shoes, she stretched out on the bed, hugging herself and wondering about the weekend ahead. The door opened and Shahknoza strutted inside, then sat on the bed pushing Orchid's legs away.

"Well, here you are Orchid. Away from all the prying eyes and here with him. Me too with Yusuf and I'm afraid at what I might do but I know God will give me strength not to do what I want to do. You too. I know what you want to do and so does he and so does Yusuf. I think Miriam and Dr. Juraeva are already doing it. Do you see how they touch when they pass each other and the looks in their eyes? It's been going on for six months now and they've been very careful because no one has seen them do anything and they can't gossip. Did you hear that music she wrote using Uzbek music on the radio last night and how they played those duets in the middle? And Salim and the doctor playing those duets and then the trios and ensembles. It was very beautiful. Where were you? I couldn't find you. I looked everywhere. Why didn't you tell me where you were going? Isn't it pleasant here? But it's so cold outside. I'm not going out there. I don't care what the doctor says about the mountain air is good for you. Yusuf feels the same. I don't know where his room is and I'm glad. I think it must be around the other corner because the doctor was guiding them down the hall and they turned right and disappeared. Let's call Miriam so she can join us. Aren't these old wooden beds nice? Look how firm these mattresses are. I bet his wife brought them from Turkey. You know they built this place by themselves".

"Shahknoz, slow down and be quiet. I can't think."
Shahknoza thumped Orchid on the leg.
"I know what you're thinking about because I know you. You're wondering if you made the right decision by coming here. So am I, but I know Yusuf and he wouldn't do anything to ruin our wedding night. Do you know Salim that well? I don't think

116

so because you haven't had that much time together. Or have you and you didn't tell me".

Orchid pushed Shahknoza to the floor then pulled her up.

"Come on, let's find Miriam".

Opening the door, they smelled an unfamiliar smell and followed it into the kitchen. Miriam and Salim wearing aprons were moving around in the kitchen. Salim had a bowl of what looked like ground beef and he was sprinkling some mustard colored powder in it. Miriam lit a funny smelling cigarette and after puffing on it, passed it to Salim, who inhaled deeply, then seeing Orchid and Shahknoza, dropped it on the counter where it went out.

"We're making you all an American Friday dinner".

Shahknoza stepped towards the kitchen but Miriam stopped her with her body.

"Off Limits Shahknoz. Go have a seat or you can watch from the outside. This is an American venture".

Shahknoza pointed to the small rolled cigarette on the counter.

"What were you smoking? It smells like burnt rags".

The two Americans doubled over in laughter and the professor entering the room with Yusuf joined them. The two Uzbek women exchanged a puzzled look.

"What's so funny?"

The doctor unrolled the joint and re-rolled it adding some herbs. He lit the joint again without the same smell, and offered it to Yusuf who inhaled and blew the smoke in Shahknoza's face.

"Would you like some dear?"

Shahknoza fanned away the smoke.

"No, and you shouldn't be smoking. Athletes need their breath".

Doctor Juraeva, Yusuf, Shahknoza and Orchid sat on the couch, the men smoking and drinking wine and the women drinking eggnog prepared by Salim.

Salim and Mariam served French fries, coleslaw, baked fish balls and shrimp chowder for dinner with hot apple pie with ice cream for dessert. The six people sat in the main room listening to music, then watched Traffic on the VCR.

The doctor stood and stretched after the movie.

'Would anyone like to go out for a walk?"

Shahknoza and Yusuf's brows wrinkled.

"Professor, it's dark outside and there are wolves in these mountains. It's dangerous to go for a walk at this time".

The professor sat down.

"I hadn't thought about that. My goodness it's late. I think I'll turn in. Good night everyone".

Miriam yawned.

"I'm tired too so I'm going to turn in".

Orchid observed the professor walk to the end of the hall and wink at Miriam, who went into her room. Yusuf rubbed Shahknoza's hand.

"Let's go out on the porch and smell the night air before we, I mean before it's time to sleep".

Shahknoza cradled Yusuf's hand and they went outside. Orchid felt her heart thumping in her chest and pulled her vest back to see if it were visible. Salim moved from the couch to the kitchen, began scraping the food from the plates, then washing the dishes. Orchid followed him but stopped at the kitchen opening.

"American men are very different from men here. An Uzbek man would never wash the dishes. He'd leave them for the women. You saw how even the professor didn't move to do anything in the kitchen".

Salim winked at her.

"We get it from our mothers. They raised us to help out with everything. That's why most of us can cook, clean, and do everything in the house".

Orchid took a drying towel from the rack and began drying the plates.

"Then what do you need a wife for?"

Salim faced her.

"Companionship."

Orchid took a large plate and ran the cloth over it.

"What do you mean by companionship??"

Salim flipped the lever allowing the water to drain then rinsed the sink with the sprayer.

"Culturally enough to be stable, but worldly enough to be sociable and adaptable".

Orchid put the dried plates in the cabinet.

"So that's companionship. Hmmm"

Salim placed some of the plates on a shelf Orchid couldn't reach.

"That's part of it. I want a partner, and a friend Orchid. Someone I can talk with and share with the way we do".

Orchid wrapped her arms around his waist from the back, putting her hand under his shirt and rubbing her fingers around his nipples. Salim faced her and something bulging from his pants throbbed against her chest. Salim lifted her, sitting her on the counter and Orchid opened her mouth and tasted his sweetness for the first time. Wrapping her arms around his neck and her legs around his waist. He carried Orchid into her room and they eased onto the bed. Orchid trembled, her body jerking. Salim stood, removed his shirt displaying his twelve pack, then lowered his pants. Orchid's limbs tingled and her eyes froze. She reached out and touched it, then tried to wrap her hand around it.

"I've never seen anything like this before".

Salim removed her hands from his organ and lay with her on the bed. Unbuttoning her sweater, he rolled it down her back, tugged at the arms getting the sweater off, lifted her inner sweater, the silk sleeveless silk garment she wore next to her skin, then unfastened her bra, removed it and smiled to himself as she put an arm across her breasts and a hand over her smooth valley.

"Don't look Salim".

Salim removed her hands.

"I'll look at you, and you at me, because that's all we're going to do, my love. I know you have to be a virgin when we get married and the sheet test is important".

Placing her hand on him he taught her pleasurable movements for him, and he for her, and they gasped and shuddered as each exploded, Orchid making oh sounds feeling his hot seed on her stomach. They wrapped around each other, sleeping and cooing until birds notified them dawn approached. Salim peaked from the door, then tiptoed to his room. Orchid touched the sticky substance on her stomach, tasted it with her finger, placing it close to her nose to smell it when the door opened and Shahknoza entered wrapped in a sheet. She plopped next to Orchid and stared at the ceiling.

"Orchid, I think I've been to heaven".

Rolling over she touched Orchid's stomach, looked at her hand, and placed Orchid's hand on her stomach.

"You too? It's sticky isn't it? Did you see it?"

Orchid covered her face with a pillow, then peeked out at Shahknoza.

"No, I didn't. I had my eyes closed".

Shahknoza removed the pillow from Orchid's face.

"it's ok Orchid. I did too but I had to see. It's a clear white. Did he lick you?"

Orchid swung the pillow at her friend.

"No, why would he do that?"

Shahknoza stretched back, showing all her teeth and touching herself between her legs.

"First he touched me right here on my button until I opened up and liquid poured from me, and then he used his tongue on the tip of it and Orchid, oh my God, I exploded and it poured out of me like a waterfall. I soaked the bed".

Turning over she spread her arms and laughed, shaking the bed.

"Wait until he does that. It's divine Orchid. And I'm still a virgin. Oh this waiting until June is going to be more difficult now that I know how good some parts of making love with him will be".

Banging on the front door made them sit up, and Shahknoza pulled up the sheet and ran from Orchid's room across the hall. Orchid slipped on her long nightgown and pulled the covers to her neck. She heard footsteps pass her door, then her aunt's voice.

"Move Ziyod. I have to get Orchid. Where is she? Let go of me. She must leave here right now".

Her door opened and auntie stood breathing hard.

"Hurry, get your clothes on. Your father will be coming here in about an hour. Someone told him you were here with these men and he's livid. Hurry.

Shahknoza, dressed, and opened her door. Auntie looked her over.

"You come too and tell Miriam to come. There's no telling what he might do so it's better no women are here. Miriam".

Miriam, emerged from around the corner carrying her bag. Orchid grabbed her clothes, stuffed them into her bag and the three women left the cabin running. Ziyod, Yusuf and Salim heard a car start, then the sound of tires spinning and moving fast. Ziyod rubbed his eyes.

"Well, we had one good night which is better than none. Let's clean our mouths and faces and get out of here. Abdullahi's a tyrant and I'd rather have it out with him at my house, not here".

Salim crossed his arms and blocked Ziyod's way.

"Why's everyone so afraid of him? We haven't done anything wrong".

Ziyod pushed past Salim.

"In his eyes you have, and that's enough. He's a powerful man in his own way and not someone you want to cross. Now hurry Salim".

Salim pointed to his bag sitting by the couch.

"I'm already ready".

He sat on the couch's arm chair and waited for the other two men to join him. Riding from the mountain towards Tashkent, Ziyod explained to Yusuf and Salim, how Abdullahi Zaynitdinova had been part of the first wave of young men to be sent to Russia to study after WWII. During this period Stalin had killed thousands of potential leaders, current leaders, and had made it a policy to indoctrinate the most brilliant young minds from Uzbekistan and all the central Asian countries by shipping them off to Russia to study after they'd been thoroughly educated in the Russian system in Uzbekistan. Abdullahi, his father and grandfather had all been singled out by the Russians but the wave after the great war was the most thorough because the war had taken many Uzbek men and women's lives and anger was everywhere. The Central Asian students were forced to live first in isolated, dilapidated dormitories, half starved, brainwashed, then slowly given better and better conditions in Moscow until they were living better than most of their fellow students. There was one restriction though; if they were caught sleeping with Russian girls, they were returned to the harsh conditions in the dorms. This presented a challenge to the Russian girls who liked the wide faced, broad backed Central Asian boys who hid their religion and fought savagely when provoked by Russian men. Abdullahi, from a religious background, had the most girls, was trained as a civil engineer, and excelling, was sent, along with his sister the doctor, by the Russians to different countries to complete their urban and rural projects. The experiences and mistreatment by the Soviets affected him and he returned to Tashkent a hardened man with zero tolerance for weakness and an orthodox view of Islam, except he developed a taste for good alcohol while he was away. He'd married an educated but religious woman from a prominent intellectual family, Orchid's mother, who didn't smoke or drink, though her brothers did, and had three children, Orchid being the oldest, Farid, her brother, coming a year later, and Gulnora three years younger. Abdullahi became the head of the engineer's union 30 years ago and it was and is his fiefdom. He was also instrumental in having the engineering university constructed, designed it and

is the president though he still teaches classes.

When independence was gained in 1991 he was

offered a ministerial position but declined,

preferring to run the university and the union. His

ties in the government and in Russia are deep, and

secretive. Ziyod smoked his pipe as they turned the

last corner to his house.

"My father was part of that first wave and he was

Abdullahi's best friend. Let me tell you the type of

men they are. Once I broke my leg riding my bike,

and my father carried me into our backyard, tied my

leg to a fence with a rope, put a stick in my mouth,

and with the other end of the rope in his hands,

pulled until my leg was set. My mother who was

watching feinted. He put two pieces of wood on

each side of my leg, wrapped the same rope around

it, and drove me to the hospital for them to put a

caste on it, crying and kissing me all the time. Every week, he'd take me to the swimming pool and throw me in the water, forcing me to swim with the caste and every week they'd have to replace the caste with a new one. My leg healed quickly though. I practiced the violin fourteen hours a day until my fingers swelled and he showed me how to soak my fingers in brine, so that the skin would thicken and squeeze pieces of rubber to strengthen my hands. I'd practice the violin, and he'd practice the piano with me, going over any part I had difficulty with, but he'd never praise me to my face. He would though praise me to their people, always within my earshot. That's how I got so good so fast. I wanted to please him and be able to be as strong as he was. He cared and bled with me through every recital, and of course, I knew all the time his real wish was for me to go to Russia, particularly St.

Petersburg where the best musicians were, and beat the Russians. The night I did, he lifted me off the floor kissing me, then rode back with me to Tashkent and dropped dead as soon as he crossed our threshold. He'd made arrangements for me to go to the west if I won the competition, and I left two weeks later, leaving my distraught mother alone. I was never so happy in my life. It took me three years to grieve for him and appreciate him. But this is what I want you to understand about Abdullahi Zaynitdinov. He tried to pressure my mother into not getting married again and remaining a widow. Guzal, Orchid's aunt who we picked up today, is still a virgin because he pressured into giving up her social life to take care of their mother".

Yusuf hiccupped with laughter.

"I don't believe a woman that beautiful and successful is still a virgin. She probably has someone she secretly sleeps with".

Salim maintained his silence, thinking about the behavior Dr. Guzal demonstrated when around men. Perspiration formed on her top lip, with her top teeth nervousing her bottom lip. She'd take short quick steps around the room, when men were present and after they'd leave, he'd hear a buzzing noise and muffled moans coming from her locked office. He'd asked his sister Miriam about it many times, but she'd told him to mind his own business and stay out of women's affairs. Ziyod emptied his pipe and opened the car door.

"If she does have a lover, no one has ever seen him or even gotten a whiff of him, or her".

The three men left the car, their heads scouring the university, looking for Abdullahi Zaynitdinov.

Three hours later, he knocked on Ziyod's door, and as Ziyod opened it, stepped inside, removed his shoes, walked into the dining room and reclined on a cushion.

"Ziyod, I'll have some of the best you have to drink. That Turkish brandy will be perfect".

Exhaling, he opened the top button of his pants and acknowledged Yusuf and Salim who stood, by touching his forehead, giving them a nod, and pointing to a cushion on the floor with an open palm. Ziyod entered the room and showed Mr. Zaynitdinov the bottle. The senior gentlemen gave him the thumbs up sign, waited until Ziyod brought him a tray with the bottle, a full glass, and took a seat across from him. Zaynitdinov inhaled the liquor, rubbed the glass between his hands, emptied the glass, then poured himself another.

"You all can drink now".

135

The three men raised their glasses to him in a salute, and sipped from the wine they'd been drinking. Zaynitdinov cleared his throat.

"Son, I think you've left out something your father had in abundance".

Ziyod jumped to his feet running from the room and returned with a small canister. The old man opened it, removed a reefer stick, smoked it half way, then chased it with a drink of brandy.

"Ahhhhh. We first planted this near the cotton fields in his village. The Soviets had sent us there as a punishment for beating up some of their workers and the assholes didn't realize it was his grandmother's village. They thought they'd brainwashed the villagers into telling on us but all we did was eat, play music, drink tea and listen to the old men and women tell stories".

Ziyod passed Yusuf and Salim a reefer.

"I didn't know you played an instrument, Uncle"

Zaynitdinov moved his first three fingers.

"I play trumpet. I just refused to play for the

Russians. Your dad and I played every day when we

were studying in the Soviet Union. That's how we

met the African Americans"

His reddened eyes focused on Salim, who held the

older man's gaze. Zaynitdinov lifted his glass.

"American Muslims are very devout and I admire

that. More so than our Tatar countrymen".

Yusuf studied his glass.

"Let me commend you young Yusuf for graduating

early and representing our country. Where will you

be playing, England or Spain?"

He smiled at Yusuf who admonished him with a

two handed raised glass.

"England. That way Shahknoz can go with me and teach the foreign players how to speak English. We're a package deal".

"Good business practice. I guess some of you Tatars do have good sense"

Ice formed in the room and Yusuf bit his thumbnail. Salim leaned forward in his chair.

"Do you say those kind of things about black people too? We have the same reputation as the Tatars in my country".

Ziyod and Yusuf slumped in their chairs and Zaynitdinov smiled showing his teeth.

"We don't have racism in Uzbekistan and that was a joke. You are a very peculiar young man. I'm grateful to you for saving my daughter's life, but your impertinence borders on disrespect which I don't tolerate".

Salim stood, and dropped to one knee.

"I meant no disrespect sir. However, you know how it feels to be joked about because of your experience with the Russians, I mean the Soviets and therefore I'd think you'd be sensitive to how it feels"

Zaynitdinov's smile dropped.

"Are you criticizing my behavior"

Salim remained on his knee.

"No sir. Who am I to criticize someone of your stature".

Zaynidinov adjusted his body and finished his drink.

"Come over here and pour me a drink".

Salim crawled on all fours and replenished the elder's drink. Orchid's father grabbed his wrist but Salim twisted loose and sat back on his knees.

Zaynitdinova sat up on his and leaned in close to Salim's ear.

"You soil my daughter's reputation by going away to the mountains alone and constantly being seen with her on campus. It must stop. Her marriage is important not only for her, but for her brother and sister. And I have already chosen a husband for her. Do you understand, American?"

Salim stroked his moustache.

"I do sir. And I respect your wishes. And Orchid's." Lowering himself again, he moved backwards across the floor, keeping his eyes on Zaynitdinov, who remained upright. Salim settled onto his cushion. Zaynitdinov licked his teeth.

"When your father, my sister and I got to Russia the African Americans were our first friends and jazz was the first common denominator. They weren't Muslims but they were Jazz lovers like we were.

Their experience was different from ours though because the Russians encouraged their girls to be close to them. They used them to recruit the black men into the party. We used to laugh together because my friends knew this and used those girls and the communist to get what they wanted; sex and a good education. We really found it humorous because as soon as my brothers returned to the U.S with their degrees, they dropped the party and lived free of their control. I guess your father never told you, Ziyod, that my sister loved one. He was a medical student like her and a saxophone player named Brandon. I approved of him and they were going to get married, but the night before they were supposed to leave for the U.S., a drunken Soviet ran over him with his car. The jackass would have killed my sister too but Brandon pushed my sister out of the way. He died instantly and the Soviets did nothing. She owes him her life and I owe you my daughter's. There's an irony here".

Lighting his joint and inhaling, he stretched back on the cushion and closed his eyes.

"Play me some Count Basie, Ziyod."

Zaynitdinov patted his feet to One O'Clock Jump, then leaping to his feet, began dancing on the rug, moving his feet and holding his hand as if he had a partner. He spun, dipped moved his hands, head, shoulders, wagging his finger in the air, then stopped as the music ended.

"My brothers taught me that. It's time to go pray. Salim, my son Farid has a fight in two months against the Russians. I want you to train him. You'll find him at the training facility. He knows who you are, and I want him to win. Ziyod, fill that container with goodies so that I may take it with me"

Ziyod took a coffee can from behind his arm cushion.

"Here, Uncle. I already prepared it for you."

Zaynitdinov kissed Ziyod on both cheeks and walked to the door.

"Yusuf, good luck and remember you represent Uzbekistan and your family at all times. Salim, I wish you all the best".

The three men watched him close the door and walk steadily across the campus towards the mosque. Salim picked up the empty fifth of Turkish brandy. He returned to his seat carrying the drained bottle. Ziyod and Yusuf sat in front of him and gave him the thumbs up sigh. Salim gave them a turned down thumb, his hands shaking. Ziyod, Yusuf and Salim pulled each other up from the floor, and Ziyod grasped Salim's shoulder.

"Come on brothers. Let's go. You marry the family".

The three exited Ziyod's home and in step caught Dr. Zaynitdinov. Linking arms, they strode to the mosque, cleaned their noses, hands, and feet, then entered the prayer room.

Salim left the group, and going into the backroom, took the microphone from a believer and did the call to prayer.

"Allah Akbar. Allah, Allah, Akbar."

As he sang, the mosque filled with men, with the women entering a separate room. Salim noticed Orchid and her mother enter the mosque, with Orchid flicking the happiness from

her eyes from recognizing Salim's voice and later seeing him sitting next to her father.

Leaving the mosque, she observed the men shaking

Salim's hands while waiting for her

father to join them. Followed by Ziyod, Yusuf and

Salim, Zyanitdinov reached Orchid

and her mother, then turned to the men behind him.

Ziyod, Yusuf, my family and I will be eating now.

You're welcome to join us".

Taking Orchid and her mother's arms, he swung the

women around, and walked

away. Orchid pivoted to look at Salim who stood

like a soldier. Ziyod and Yusuf locked

arms with Salim. Ziyod placed his pipe in his

mouth.

"Let's go eat brothers."

Orchid's father's voice claimed her attention.

"The path to our home is in front of you Orchid".

Orchid blinked twice at Salim, their signal for I love

you, and walked out of step with her parents.

CHAPTER FOUR

Orchid and Auntie Guzal strode arm in arm, their heads high, braving the wind making their hair swirl. Seriousness weighed on their shoulders but they carried it with ease, and gained strength from it. Reaching Orchid's father and Guzal's brother's house on the edge of the campus, Auntie kissed Orchid on the forehead.

"Are you ready? Keep it short because the more he talks, the more irrational he becomes".

Entering the house, Orchid's mother met her at the door and embracing her daughter, then her sister in law motioned her hand like someone was drinking something. The two women spun their fingers in the air. Orchid entered the living room first, shoeless and first kissed her father, then her brother. Auntie sat facing her brother on the floor after Farid had kissed her.

"Papa, you wanted to talk to me".

Zayntdinova clasped and unclasped his hands.

"Have you done anything which will bring me shame?"

Orchid, on her knees in front of him, placed her hands in a prayer position.

"Never papa. You know me better".

"I thought I did, but you've been behaving rather strangely."

Orchid sat back and crossed her legs.

"I have not."

Farid smacked his arm cushion.

"You have. You're always with those Americans and especially qirivchi, the bear killer and people are gossiping about you."

Orchid pointed her finger at him.

"You'd rather listen to gossip than ask me. What kind of brother are you? You should be defending me rather than listening to them. I'm your sister and you know me".

Farid opened and closed his mouth.

"I do defend you, but I shouldn't have to"

Orchid twirled an end of her hair, picking up her auntie's signal to calm down.

"If you know me brother then you don't have to. We've never gone anywhere without a chaperon and I've done nothing wrong because I'm with the man I love. I want to marry him, papa".

Zaynitdinov raised his eyes to Orchid's mother standing in the doorway. She entered the room and placed a tray of smoking tea in the middle.

"Let's all drink tea and speak to each other like a family".

They all took tea cups and sipped from them. Zaynitdinov held his cup and stared into it.

"From all reports he's a good student, a warrior, a Muslim and a good man. However, he has no natural family, and what will your marrying him do for your brother and sister? And what does he have to offer, daughter?"

"A bright future better than any man from this country can offer her."

Auntie placed her cup on the small table beside her. Zaynitdinov slurped his tea, his face turning to stone.

"And I guess you know this because you are his professor?"

Auntie faced her brother.

"Yes, and because I work with him every day and I know he does have a family. A Muslim family. Yes, he and his sister were adopted, but they are a family and they're all physicians. Plus, I've watched him closely and he, they, have integrity, and will be very successful surgeons".

Her brother placed his tea on the table to his right.

"Are you sure you aren't seeing someone else when you look at him? Someone you lost?"

Auntie got to her feet and strode to the door.

"How dare you Abdullahi? But to answer your question, no I'm not projecting and I'm sure about this man".

Orchid's mother rose and pulled Auntie down onto the carpet next to Orchid. Zaynitdinov rubbed his palms.

"I just needed to hear that from you. But Orchid, I've made my decision and found someone for you.

I've arranged for you two to go out on a date. At least do that".

"No papa. I know who I love and want to be with."

Her brother leaned forward his face almost touching his sister's.

"You disrespect papa and defy his wishes so easily?"

Orchid raised her chin.

"I mean no disrespect, but yes, I love Salim and if I have to defy papa over this, I will."

Orchid's mother shrugged her shoulders at her husband. Zaynitdinov played a finger rhythm on both thighs, stood and exited the living room with Farid following him.

"So be it, Orchid. But don't bring him here".

Her head up, Orchid used both middle fingers to block the tears in the corners of her eyes. Her mother helped her to stand.

"Give him time Orchid. He's just upset because Salim wasn't his choice. Men are like that. Especially him. Now go study".

Kissing her mother on both cheeks, Orchid and Auntie Guzal departed her parents' house and allowed the wind to move them along. Orchid opened her arms letting the wind carry her and she glided like a bird moving through the sky, dipping and moving with the breeze, her voice calling Salim's name. Auntie walked behind Orchid watching her, and shouted Brandon into the wind, telling him she missed him, and the two women separated, each heading to their domiciles, and throwing kisses to each other as they did.

CHAPTER FIVE

Orchid, Salim and Farid sat inside the gymnasium's viewing room watching the Russian fighter's films. She marveled at the tree trunk now sitting beneath her brother's head and the boulders protruding from his chest. She knew, and Farid knew his physique and new attention to detail was attributable to Salim who'd trained Farid by having him cut down trees with an ax, pull an old 1940's WWII jeep up a hill, run wearing ankle weights and arm weights up hills, box with weights on both arms in the swimming pool, hold weights on his head lifting them up and down and chasing chickens around a yard trying to capture them. His back muscles bulged when he extended his arm across a chair and Orchid also knew, as Farid did, that they were the result of his holding pulling horses with a harness strapped around his back. Salim ran the film backwards and paused it.

"What do you notice?"

Farid dropped his left hand and stuck out his neck.

"He keeps his left hand low and whenever he gets ready to throw a left jab he sticks his neck out".

"Anything else?"

Farid laughed.

"Whenever he gets ready to throw an over hand right he plants his left and raises his right foot up on the ball of his foot. Actually up to his toe and he has trouble with lateral movement. If I stand in front of him he'll drop me so I have to keep moving and firing my shot gun in his face, arm, elbow, chest and especially to his upper arm like Marciano did to Jersey Joe Walcott".

Orchid clapped and Farid ruffled his sister's hair. Salim turned off the film and flipped on the lights.

"Okay, one more open hand sparring session but without the weights".

Orchid walked in front of her brother and Salim and listened to Salim repeat the same words he'd drilled into Farid's head every day for the past two months; Russians were stand up fighters who always fought tall using their height but they sacrificed speed for power because they threw their jabs from their waist. At least these fighters did and that Farid should expect anything on fight night. Orchid looked at the ripples of muscle on her brother's legs as he climbed into the ring and she knew, besides the running, they were the result of the thousand kicks in both legs Salim had had Farid do every day. Inside and outside the ring, six different tall and lean lightweight boxers waited their turn to spar open handed with Farid who bristled, his eyes turning to glass when he stepped into the ring. Farid shouted "lean and mean" and "stick and dip" and the light weights charged her brother. Orchid yelled into the ring.

"Hear the music Farid and move your head to it. They can't hit what they can't find. Dance to it".

Farid moved his hands and feet, circling, giving them angles and blocking their rapid punches with his shoulders, elbows and forearms. Each of the light weights went down and after twelve five minute rounds, Salim told Farid to practice retreating legs. Farid ran backwards around the ring in circles and in angles for forty-five more minutes before he was stopped. Climbing down from the ring with his trunks sweat shirt and socks soaked, he gave Salim a bear hug.

"Thank you for everything brother. I keep apologizing to you for believing bad words about you and I know they weren't true. I've been talking to father about you every day and he listens but says nothing. I know though that he's coming around. What shall I do tomorrow?"

Salim faked a punch at Farid who raised his arm to block the punch and ducked. Salim kissed Farid on the cheek.

"Go swimming, get to bed early and don't have any negative conversations. And remember the day of the fight eat a hearty breakfast, a light lunch and a big salad in the early evening and drink your ginseng and honey. You should have a good bowel movement a good hour before the fight. Orchid and Auntie will do the rest".

The two men slapped fives and Farid walked to the shower. Orchid leaned against Salim, feeling the mound growing in his pants and standing on her tiptoes, pulled his head down to taste his mouth, then stopped, the hair rising on her arms. Her

mother stood in the doorway next to Auntie Guzal.

"Mother, what are you doing here?"

Her mother walked to her with open arms.

'I've come to see my daughter and bring her home

with me. You know what day it is?"

Orchid's stomach turned.

"It's papa's birthday. I have a present for him".

Salim bowed to Orchid's mother.

"And so do I."

He left the room and returned with a square package

which he handed to Orchid's

mother.

"Be careful, it's a little heavy".

Mrs. Zaynitdinova held the package with both

hands.

"It is heavy. What's in it?"

Salim bowed again, this time extending his arms.

"The complete recordings of the Count Basie band from its beginnings in Kansas City until the end. I hope he'll like them."

The mother ran her hand across the package and sat it on the floor. Gazing at Salim, she took three quick steps and ran the back of her hand across his cheek.

"You are a very kind man. I'm sorry for what my husband has done".

She back pedaled to the package and wept on Auntie Guzal's shoulder. Orchid, and Auntie Guzal exchanged eye brows dipped downwards, confused looks and comforted the crying woman's back. Salim exhaled.

"Enjoy your father's birthday, my love. I have to go to work because I'm on call tonight. I'll see you tomorrow ok? Dr. Guzal, I'll see you later tonight".

Blowing Orchid a kiss, which she caught and returned, he left the gymnasium and high fived Farid who passed him.

Orchid, her mother, auntie and Farid skipped across the campus to her parents' house. Once inside, she and Farid greeted all the university professors and Orchid cornered Ziyod once the evening was in full swing with people drinking punch, eating and the men sharing alcohol concealed in punch and soda. Farid kissed his father, gave him his gift and went upstairs to bed. Ziyod, eyes red and a bit closed leaned down to hear Orchid.

"My mother's being very emotional and look she's talking. That's unusual. What's going on?"

Ziyod turned and watched Orchid's mother moving from group to group.

"Long marriages always get more sentimental with years and birthdays remind people of how time flies. Think about it Orchid, she was just a girl just graduating from college when they were married and they've aged together. Plus, she knows what's occurring between you two and it saddens her because he's her husband, you're her daughter and she knows what a catch Salim is. This situation would upset any mother"

Orchid agreed and listened to the sky rumbling.

"You're right and it is upsetting. Farid says my papa's coming around though. If he wins on Friday, that will seal the deal. Salim taught me that expression".

People began to sing a song for Orchid's dad and she moved to the front of the crowd, going to her father, kissing him and warming to the firm hug and kiss he placed on her forehead. Lifting her hair over her shoulders, a knot formed in Orchid's throat when he whispered I love you and I'd do anything for you in her ear. He then sighed and thanked her for the Count Basie records. Orchid throat dried, contracted, and a squeaky inaudible sound came from her throat.

"It's from both of us papa".

Her father didn't hear her over the singing and laughter.

The day of the fight, Orchid, light headed with happiness from the mink coat Salim had had sent to her room, entered the clinic untying the gold silk scarf he'd also given her. He sat behind his desk squeezing tennis balls and watching the snow fall in sheets from the window.

"My, don't you look like a fresh star in the night. Where'd you get that mink coat from?"

Orchid closed the door and sat on his lap.

"I don't know. I think a generous man who loves me bought it for me. Do you know him?"

Salim adjusted Orchid on his lap.

"I think I might. He's kind of crazy and in love with her".

Their mouths warmed each other's and Orchid clamped her legs feeling the wetness growing within her. She jumped from his lap, pulling the coat around her hearing a knock at the door. Auntie peeked her head in the door.

"Oh my goodness. What a beautiful coat".

Orchard spun around modeling her coat.

"My baby bought it for me. Auntie, I know your face, you knew already. I bet you brought it back from Russia when you were there".

Auntie sang Isaac Hayes *I Stand Accused* and pretended to spank herself. Salim looked at his watch.

"Okay you two, it's time to work with Farid. I'll see you there".

He kissed both women and saw them to the door. Orchid and Auntie Guzal skipped

across the campus passing the people hunched over walking through the steady snow. Entering the arena which was already full, they went to the room where Farid was stretched out on a massage table and his father sat in a chair next to him. Orchid opened a cabinet behind the table and near the door and sat the VCR on a pile of books. Auntie inserted the disk and turned off the lights. Farid sat up.

"What are you doing? I don't feel like watching a movie. I have to fight in a few minutes."

Mr. Zaynitdinova used his fingertips to push his son flat onto the table. The film showed Russian soldiers shooting Uzbek men during one of the rebellions, raping Uzbek women, skeletal Uzbek children and fat Russian soldiers taunting the children by holding the food above them, out of reach, then swallowing some and throwing the rest at them which made them fight for the food. The film ended and Auntie turned on the light. Farid's neck muscles contracted, he pounded his gloves into each other, and when the Uzbek coach entered the room wearing the body guard for punching, Farid pressed him against the wall with punches until the coach begged him to stop. A three knock signal on the door echoed around the room and they left the room following Farid and his coach. Their father moved his lips in and out. Reaching the arena, Orchid and auntie found their seats next to her mother, Ziyod, Miriam, Yusuf and Shahknoza.

Looking around they waited for Salim. Farid

ascended the steps to the ring and stepped through

the ropes into the ring. He shimmied his upper

torso, arms, legs, snapped his neck to both sides,

pointed at his family and not seeing Salim, stopped.

The announcer made the introductions, the trainer

removed Farid's robe but he still searched the

audience for Salim. The bell rang and the Russian

rushed across the ring as Farid turned and ducked

without raising his arm. The blow glanced off

Farid's head knocking him to the canvas. Farid

shook his head taking the eight count when from the

audience people heard a voice shouting "lean and

mean, stick and dip. He can't hit what he can't

find." Orchid and the group picked up the chant and

Farid danced into the center of the ring shooting his

shotgun jab connecting every punch to the Russians

body and head. After four rounds the Russian could barely lift his left arm and his left eye was a purple blob. Farid closed in flicking left jabs and then threw four over hand rights which knocked the Russian through the ropes, his upper body sprawled onto the announcer's table with his legs and feet in the ring twitching, urine dripping onto the mat.

The crowd and the family jumped to their feet and Farid saluted the crowd by blowing kisses then walked to his corner and was pointing down at Salim when his face contorted and his mouth turned into a straight line. Orchid turned to see what had made her brother make such an ugly face. Five men in full length black leather coats, hats and gloves walked down the aisle and pointed at Salim. Salim pointed to himself and they nodded yes. He moved down the aisle in front of them and the men grabbed him and almost lifted his feet off the ground, moved him down the aisle. Orchid's mother began to wail and her father crossed his arms, staring straight ahead at Farid. Auntie looked down at her crying sister-in-law.

"You knew about this and that's what you meant when he gave you the gift for my brother. You bitch".

She ran from the arena followed by Miriam, Ziyod, Yusuf, and Shahknoza. They arrived outside in time to see the men putting handcuffs on Salim who spit on the ground. Auntie Guzal moved close to the police men.

"I'm Dr. Guzal Zaynitdinova and this man works with me in my clinic. My brother is"
"We know who your brother is doctor".
Auntie brushed the snow from her face.
"Then tell me why you're arresting him".

The head man removed his dark glasses and pulled an envelope from his coat pocket.

"We found these drugs in his dorm room under his pillow. He's being deported right now."

Miriam lunged at the men but was restrained by Ziyod.

"Deported? For what? Those aren't his drugs. He'd never be stupid enough to leave anything in his room. This is a set up. Who told you they were there? Did you do this Yusuf?"

Yusuf's shoulders pulled back.

"I'd never do something like this to my friend. Who told you about the drugs officer?"

The officer looked above them and towards the arena.

"We had an anonymous tip from a reliable source. And for your information it was not this young man.

We want to protect him from this American drug

dealer."

Miriam stamped her feet.

"If my brother goes I go".

Salim spit again.

"Don't sister. You only have a few more months

here so finish it out. You know I'll be alright. I

know who's behind this and it isn't brother Yusuf

or anyone here. I'll be alright sister. Orchid, I love

you".

The policemen pushed Salim to a waiting van, and

pushing his head down threw him inside, slammed

the door and pulled away throwing snow. A crowd

stood and watched whispering. Orchid couldn't feel

her knees and reached out for Yusuf who caught her

along with Ziyod. Miriam kicked snow and cursed

sending the snow in the direction the van had left.

Auntie, her eyes wide and blazing turned to go

inside the arena and halted. Farid stood with his arms around he and Orchid's parents. Orchid's mother covered her face. Auntie approached them.

"Why Abdullahi? Why? He's not only a brilliant and gifted surgeon, he's a kind and good human being who loves your daughter more than anything in his life. And you with your pride did this to him and to her. I spit on you".

She let a wad fly and it landed on her brother's jacket.

"And you coward, user, Farid, you knew about this and probably put those drugs under his pillow. How could you? How could you when you know without him you couldn't have won that fight? You will never have love and peace in your life for doing this".

Farid shuffled his feet in the snow. Zaynitdinov moved his family past the crowd and spoke over his shoulder at his sister.

"Go home and embarrass us no more in public Guzal. This is family business."

Auntie surveyed the crowd and taking Orchid's arm tried to move her but Orchid's legs wouldn't move. Yusuf and Ziyod lifted Orchid and carried her across the campus and to the clinic where they deposited her on the bed. Miriam, Shahknoza and auntie Guzal sat with Orchid. Auntie left the room and returned with some smelling salt.

"You guys leave. We'll take care of her".

The two men left murmuring to each other. Auntie moved the bottle under Orchid's nose but she still stared at the door. Auntie then gave her an injection.

"She'll be asleep in a minute and should be alright in the morning. Come back tomorrow. She's in shock".

The two women departed, Orchid closed her eyes, then curled into a fetal position.

She awoke with fog covering her eyes in the darkness. Looking at her watch which glowed in the darkness, a watch he'd bought for her, he being Salim, she rolled out of the bed and sat her feet on the cold tile. Salim always rubbed her feet in the mornings, and made sure her lamb wool slippers were next to her bed so that she wouldn't have to place her feet on the tile which she didn't like. He'd have come into her room if they were sleeping at Ziyod's before she awakened and did this for her. And since it was five thirty, he would already be in Ziyod's kitchen stirring the fruit smoothie because he wouldn't want to wake anyone in the house.

He'd be stretching in the kitchen, drinking his ginseng with hot water and looking out the window humming some oldies song, or some melody he'd be hearing. She loved that he sang or hummed all the time, telling her he heard music in his head 24/7, and that he moved his fingers all the time because he played the melodies on his horn, unable to play because of his work. She laughed out loud remembering how he told her he made music doing surgery, feeling the melodies as he worked on people's bodies. Tiptoeing on the clinic floor she found the toilet and sat there recalling how Salim would stand outside the door singing to her as she used the toilet. She, laughing, once told him to go away because using the toilet was private, and heard his voice trailing away and coming from another room as he waited for her. And upon opening the door she found a flower in a small vase with an

175

incense stuck inside. Giggling she'd gotten the message and had sat the vase with the incense inside the toilet. Leaving the toilet, dawn opened a weary eye and if Salim were here they'd be outside doing a few warm up exercises before they'd begin their run, and during their run Salim's head would scan the area, aware of everything around him and if anyone appeared he'd pull her behind him, poised to defend her or attack if necessary. Shahknoz, Yusuf, Miriam and Ziyod would join them on their run, which they'd do in silence, then return to Ziyod's house for a vegetable or fruit smoothie and some warm granola for Salim and Miriam, eggs and sausage and something Salim had sent to him from America called grits which she, Shahknoz and Yusuf loved, with butter and pepper. It filled the stomach and warmed the insides along with the tea Yusuf made for everyone. Entering the room, she'd been in, she looked at the lean figure sitting in the chair next to her bed, the back straight, head up with bushy hair she fluffed out with a pick. It was Miriam and Orchid knew she was there because she was on duty taking over for her auntie, and because of last night. Miriam turned to her and waited until Orchid sat on the edge of the bed.

"Are you alright Orchid?"

Orchid reached for her purse and opening it, took out her tooth brush, holding it up. "Always be prepared for unprepared situations". They said this in unison and laughed together.

"He'd say that all the time, and I guess this is one of them. Yes, I'm alright, but I don't think I'll ever be alright without him".

Miriam patted Orchid on the knee and Orchid returned the concern.

"I should be asking you the same Miriam. How are you?"

Miriam crossed her legs. One almost touching the floor.

"I'm angry. I never thought something like this would happen. And what's funny, and as you know, he hadn't even been sleeping in that dorm room because he'd been staying at Ziyod's most of the time. That's the irony of this situation".

Orchid found her heels and clacked to the bathroom where she cleaned her mouth, then returned to the room. It was getting lighter and Miriam's puckered mouth was visible.

"Who would do this to him Orchid? It's vicious"

"My father".

Miriam shifted in the chair and worried her forehead.

"I feel for you and I wouldn't want to be in the position you're in".

A red light flashed above the door and Miriam scurried from the room. Orchid slipped on her jacket and passed Miriam, orderlies and other doctors pushing a gurney with a bleeding farmer into double doors. Salim would love this, she thought to herself while buttoning the coat he'd bought for her. She pulled the collar up sniffing it for a whiff of his cologne, then heard her name being called. She knew that voice. Siroj reached Orchid and halted her by tugging at her arm. Orchid gave his hand her attention and he released her arm.

"I know you don't trust me Orchid, and I can only apologize. You of all people shouldn't judge people."

Orchid stopped walking.

"I haven't judged you. I just haven't forgotten what you did".

Siroj pulled his jacket tighter and their breath was visible in the air.

"We've been friends all our lives and I'm still your friend. Our families are friends."

Orchid wiped the cold running from her nose with a silk handkerchief with her and Salim's initials on it.

"This is true. Why did you stop me Siroj?"

Siroj handed her an envelope.

"Because as a friend I want to share these with you".

Orchid took the envelope and placed it in her purse.

"What is it?"

Siroj took two steps from her.

"It's one friend sharing with another".

Bending forward and into the now flurrying snow, he left Orchid fingering her purse.

Orchid pulled her gold scarf over her head and moved through the snow flakes to Ziyod's house. The door opened before she could knock and Shahknoz pulled her inside.

"Oh Orchid I was so worried about you. You couldn't speak last night and you were acting like a zombie. We were shaken. Are you alright? Salim called a few minutes ago. He's still in Moscow. They put him on a plane but they didn't stamp deported on his passport. He said he felt you and he'll call back. Look at all the snow. Yusuf prepare her some tea. I don't know what's going on but something's not right. Do you think your father did this? What are you going to do?"

Yusuf stepped between Shahknoza and Orchid. "Shahknoz. Give her a minute to get inside." Shahknoza used her hip to move Yusuf out of the way.

"You go make tea, man."

Yusuf, his chest sunken, went into the kitchen.

Ziyod joined Orchid and Shaknoza in the living

room and once she'd reclined, he kissed her on the

forehead.

"Are you alright?"

Orchid made the so so sign. Ziyod tore off the top

sheet of a pad he held.

"I wrote down what Salim said. Here."

Orchid read the words I love my dearest. And when

you graduate, if you still want to be together, I'll

send you a ticket to come to America and we'll be

together forever. I have enough money in the bank

to sponsor you. Start the application process now.

I'll call you at Ziyod's house when I arrive home".

Orchid kissed the paper, folded it and placed it in

her bra, close to her heart. Shaknoza tickled

Orchid's foot.

"See, everything will work out. Sometimes pain makes beauty more appreciated. What will you do about your family though Orchid?"

Orchid rubbed her heart.

"I'll know when the time comes".

Yusuf placed the tea in front of them and they all drank, waiting for the phone to ring. Orchid opened her purse and took out the envelope. Shahknoza eyed it.

"What's that? I feel something evil coming from it."

Orchid brushed Shaknoza's words away with a flick of her hand.

"Shahknoz, it's only an envelope Siroj just gave to me."

Shahknoza leaned back.

"Then I know it's evil."

Yusuf and Ziyod winked at each other and tried not to laugh and spit out their tea. Orchid opened the envelope, removed the pictures and held her breathe. Shahknoza leaned over, looking down at the pictures and covered her eyes. Orchid, now breathing spread the five photographs on the carpeted floor. Each was a snapshot of auntie Guzal and Salim in intimate moments. She on top of him, then against the wall, bent over on his desk, backwards on his lap in a chair and on the floor. Ziyod dropped his tea cup and Yusuf stood and paced the room, swinging his fists in the air.

"He deceived us. He deceived us all".

Shahknoza, water leaking from her eyes and nose, pulled Orchid to her.

"And right under our noses. Oh Orchid, I'm so sorry." She planted kisses around Orchid's face and head. Orchid used balled fists to pound her thighs, but was interrupted by the phone. Ziyod answered it.

"Yes, she's here".

He handed Orchid the phone and studied the pictures. Orchid, ashen faced and glass eyed, took the phone.

"Before you say anything you lying cheating, despicable animal, I saw the pictures. We've all seen them and they're right here in front of us".

She held the phone away from her ear allowing everyone to hear Salim's voice.
"What pictures? What are you talking about and why are you calling me names?"
Orchid moved the phone closer.
"The pictures of you and my aunt in the clinic. Don't try and deny it. We're looking at them now.

You've been having sex with her all this time you bastard."

"I've never had sex with your aunt. That's despicable. You're my fiancée and she's your family. I'd never do something like that and you should know me better my love".

Orchid placed the phone on the carpet.

"I thought I knew you. We all did, but you fooled us. Never call me again. I hate you".

She threw the phone to Ziyod, who took it into the next room. They could hear his voice, but couldn't understand what was being said.

Orchid rose and went to the door. Reaching for her coat, her hand touched it, then recoiled.

"Ziyod. I need a coat and a scarf to go outside. I don't want anything of his to touch me".

Ziyod emerged from the back carrying a full length wool coat and a wide scarf.

"These were hers. I hope you won't mind wearing them".

Ziyod helped Orchid into the coat.

"Look. I know you're upset but there must be an explanation. This isn't like him. Plus, look at the weather Orchid. It's almost a blizzard. Please, don't go out there."

Orchid pushed past Ziyod.

"There are no explanations and I have to be with my family".

Opening the door, she wrapped the scarf around her face and braved the sheets of snow. Arriving at the University of Engineering, she shook the snow from her clothes like a dog releasing water and climbed the steps lead footed to her father's office. Opening the door and walking past his secretary she opened her father's door and closing it went to her father who looked out the window with his back to the door.

"Did you know about the photographs papa?"

He fastened his hand into Orchid's.

"Yes, daughter I did. And that it's my sister makes it worse. God help us as a family if people find out."

Orchid kissed her father's hand.

"They won't papa. I know how to handle Siroj and we won't let this damage our family because we're a family. Let's agree not to say anything to auntie, mother or Farid".

Her head on his shoulder they watched the snow until her father's secretary signaled him it was time for his meeting. The father and daughter left the office together.

Orchid struggled through the blizzard, thinking while walking she heard Miriam's voice calling her. Arriving at her dorm room, she dialed Siroj's number and waited until he answered.

"Thank you for the pictures. That's something a friend would do. When the storm subsides we'll go out on that date you've always wanted to have which will start the ball rolling for what you and my father want. Ok?"

Not waiting for Siroj to answer she hung up the phone and climbed into her bed fully dressed.

The phone rang three times then clicked off. It rang again, clicked off, then rang again. Orchid answered it.

"Orchid, this is Miriam. I know you think I'm defending my brother but I looked at those pictures and that's not his body. Listen to me Orchid. You know he has a scar on the left side of his body near his waist and it's not there on the picture. And that's not your aunt's body either. I've seen her naked. Listen to me Orchid. I can have your aunt verify it."

Orchid let Miriam hear her breathing.

"You and my aunt would say anything and pictures sometimes obscure things so I don't believe you. This is my family and I'll handle my aunt my own way so you stay out of it. If you show her those pictures my father will have you deported in minutes. Now stay away from us, you liar. You're just like your brother".

Hanging up the phone she called her father's office and he answered.

"Papa, deport Miriam Salim's sister now. She's going to interfere with our family".

Orchid placed the phone on the floor besides her bed and waited to hear the police sirens. Within five minutes she heard them moving across the campus, then again a few minutes later. Closing her eyes and sitting up she removed her wet boots and seeing her reflection in the mirror, threw a boot at the mirror breaking it. Shahknoza opened her door and entered, then left the room and returned wearing her shoes and carrying a broom and dustpan. After sweeping up the glass, she squatted beside Orchid's bed. Orchid placed an open palm in front of her friend's face.

"Either you're with me or you're with them Shahknoz. It's either or".

Shahknoza pushed herself up and stood over Orchid.

"I'm your best friend and I'm always with you. But you may be wrong. I can't take this Orchid. It doesn't feel good to me. Yusuf used his influence to help me petition for early graduation and when I went to the dean, he said yes so I'm going to take all my exams tomorrow. Then Yusuf and I are going to get married and by Friday I'll be in England with him and starting my new life. I hope you'll come to the wedding. It will be in Yusuf's village. If you don't come, I'll understand".

Shahknoza carried the broom and dustpan full of broken glass to the door and opening it looked outside.

"You're my best friend and I love you like the sister I've never had. And I'm with you. But I feel you're wrong".

Orchid picked up her shoe and threw it at Shahknoza who'd closed the door.

CHAPTER SIX

Three days later Orchid rode with Shahknoza and her aunt to Yusuf's village twenty miles outside Tashkent. They exited the car and were greeted by the taxi driver who always parked in front and Fatima, superbly clothed with her hair done and teeth in her mouth. Orchid and Shahknoza peered at Fatima.

"Do you know Yusuf?"

Fatima cackled.

"Know him? He's my son and this is his brother Zaid. Welcome to our family Shahknoza".

Shahknoza staggered backwards then composed herself.

"Why didn't you tell us? We've known you years".

Fatima placed Shahknoza's hands between hers.

"How else would I know how my future daughter in law is and how she would be with my son. Now come inside. Yusuf is waiting".

Orchid and Shahknoza's aunt stood with her during the ceremony because both Shahknoza's parents were deceased. Her aunt had to sit down several times because she was too old to stand for long periods. They danced and sang throughout the evening and Orchid tasted alcohol for the first time. Yusuf encountered her after she'd helped Shahknoza's aunt go to bed.

"Thank you for coming Orchid. It means everything to Shahknoz. Her aunt won't be here much longer and she feels like you're the only family she has".

Orchid cupped his face between her hands.

"I feel the same and she's closer to me than my own sister. I know you'll be good to her because she'll be good to you".

Yusuf drank from his champagne and opened his mouth. Orchid cupped his mouth.

"Please Yusuf. I don't want to talk about it".

"But Orchid. Siroj is"

Orchid left Yusuf standing and joined Shahknoza on the dance floor, staying there until the party ended. She rode with Shahknoza and Yusuf to the airport alone because Fatima refused to go. Orchid didn't want to release Shahknoza and used her dress to clean her and Shahknoza's face.

"I'll miss you Shahknoz. I don't know how I'm going to make it without you. Call me and tell me how it is".

Shahknoz pinched Orchid's nose.

"I will if I can walk. I'll miss you too Orchid and I know you don't want to hear this but look at those pictures again. Promise me. Ok?"

Orchid pulled Shahknoza's hair.

"If I had them I might. I destroyed them Shahknoz".

Shahknoza wiped Orchid's running eyeliner with her hand.

"The truth will find you. No matter what you do, Orchid. Farewell and I'll call you from England".

Orchid watched Shahknoz and Yusuf enter the passenger's area and ride up the escalator.

CHAPTER SEVEN

Three months later Orchid stood before her father in the hallway outside the auditorium where she was getting married. Her father kissed Orchid on the forehead.

"You've graduated, you're getting married and you can now buy your own bread".

Orchid knelt before her father.

"Thank you for everything, papa. I defied you and I'm glad you showed me the truth. I love you, papa".

Her father helped her rise and escorted her down the aisle where Siroj awaited her.

Later sitting at the table with Siroj, auntie Guzal approached her and pulled her up from the table, dragging her outside in the courtyard and away from everyone

"Congratulations on marrying the wrong man and ruining your life. I hope you'll be happy in the shit you've thrown yourself into".

Auntie staggered away. Orchid gave her the finger. "As if you didn't have something to do with it?" Auntie spun on her heel.

"You think I don't know about what you believe and what you did to Miriam. You're crazy if you think I'd ever sleep with my niece's fiancé or anyone I work with. I'm not like your father and I piss on you."

She spread her legs, squatted and urinated.

"This is for you, your life, our family, and the incompetent sleaze you just married. I curse you Orchid. I curse you and until you investigate and

learn the truth, you'll never be happy. My curse
starts now".

Auntie pulled off her soiled panties and threw at
Orchid. Orchid let the panties hit the ground and
kicked them away from her. Hearing her mother's
voice, she picked them up, rolled them into a ball
and hid them under her dress.

"What are you doing out here Orchid?"
Her mother fiddled with Orchid's hair. You look
like you've seen a ghost."
Orchid held her mother's arm for support.
"I did. Drunk Auntie Guzal".
Her mother scoffed.
"That witch is just frustrated seeing you get married
because the train passed her by and no one has ever
penetrated her wall. I bet there's cobwebs down
there".

Orchid fanned her mother.

199

"Mother. I've never heard you talk like that."

Her mother moved Orchid to a corner and held her shoulders.

"When he comes to you tonight, try and relax. If you have to, sip some wine so you can stay calm because if you get nervous and tighten up. It will hurt more".

Orchid returned her mother's grasp.

"Will it hurt?"

"Yes, daughter, it's a pain you'll never forget, but it's a sweet pain. If he licks you down there it will be easier but I don't think he will. He's not that kind of man. Salim was".

Orchid pulled her mother close.

"Yes he was and he already licked me down there. Whenever he touched me I gushed out. I feel nothing with Siroj".

Her mother backed away.

"I know. You've done this for your father, brother and sister. And something else you won't tell me that only you and your father share. It's okay. I don't want to know. Blessings daughter".

Orchid bowed touching her forehead against her mother's feet and after a kiss on the top of her skull, she rose and they reentered the wedding festivities.

....

Later, Siroj and Orchid entered his father's house. He carried her up the stairs and into the bedroom. Siroj removed her clothes and looked at Orchid in only her bra and panties.

'Let me take a shower first, Siroj".

Orchid stayed in the shower moistening herself, and then she exited, wearing only a towel wrapped around her. Siroj showered and exited the bath, a towel wrapped around his bottom parts. Orchid, who'd drank a lot from a bottle of wine, pulled back the covers and removing the towel, closed her eyes and lay back on the bed. Siroj laid next to her and kissed her. Orchid opened her eyes and looked down.

"It's not standing."

Siroj looked at himself.

"I know. I don't know what's wrong"

Orchid took his organ in her hands, stroked it, rubbed it against her, then licked it. Siroj pushed her head back.

"Don't do that. That's dirty. Is that what the American taught you?"

Orchid rubbed his chest and down to his testicles.

"The American never touched me. This is for you because you're my husband and only we share this."

Siroj closed his eyes but nothing happened. There was a knock on the door. Siroj sat up.

"Who is it?"

"Fatima. It's time for me to check the sheet but I feel something. Open the door".

Orchid wrapped a sheet around her and Siroj put on a robe. Fatima entered the room, looked at the sheet and taking out her teeth, sniffed the air.

"Where are the soiled panties?"

Orchid watched her eyes rolling up to the whites.

"Inside my purse."

Fatima opened Orchid's purse, took out the panties and lifting her dress, stuck them in the behind part of her panties. She then went into the bathroom and called to Orchid who entered it.

"Did any of your family members visit this house before you got married?"

Orchid thought.

"My mom and my aunt Guzal."

Fatima sniffed the air again and bending down put her hand under the sink and removed a pair of bloody panties. Orchid covered her nose from the stink.

"I didn't smell that before Fatima."

Fatima led Orchid out of the room and pushed her onto the bed. Orchid fell backwards, then sat up, her feet over the side. Fatima opened Orchid's legs and taking a pocket knife from her bra, made a slit in the mattress, put her hand inside and pulled out a piece of yellowed paper with writing on it. Holding the paper away from her, she picked up the Koran from atop the dresser and began reading it while walking around the room. Siroj began to perspire, then collapsed onto the bed, his organ exposed. Fatima read some more, and backed out the room, giving Orchid a toothless smile accompanied by a wink. Siroj snored for a few minutes and Orchid watched his organ rise and stand at twelve o'clock. The thought crept in, but shaking her head she washed it away.

He isn't half Salim's size.

She finished the small bottle of wine and taking the now awake Siroj by the organ, guided him into her and screamed when her wall was broken. Siroj finished quickly, and Fatima knocked again, came inside, pulled the bloody sheet from the bed and left the room, displaying the sheet to the family members in the house. Laying together, Siroj came to her again twice that night, then slept, his breathing easily. Rubbing her hands over his slim shoulders, she recalled how her hands couldn't spread across Salim's, and how she always slept before him. Touching herself, she moved until her reservoir emptied, as she'd done in front of Salim, then pouring out in front of each other, and how she'd slept on his chest, feeling the curls which circled his nipples. Moving her fingers again, she exploded, placing her hand into her mouth, stifling the sound, and was then able to sleep. The next morning, sore and walking with measured steps, Orchid called Shahknoza.

"My wedding night was successful, but not like yours".

Shahknoza gave her usual cackle.

"I knew that. You were dry and it hurt like hell. That's because you don't love him."

Orchid heard the phone click.

Two weeks later, she missed her cycle, and realized in nine months she'd be a mother.

BOOK TWO

CHAPTER EIGHT

Orchid waddled into the room holding her watermelon sized stomach and grunting sat on the side of her grandmother's bed. Her grandmother opened her eyes, the glaze which covered them shining. Orchid took a wet cloth and wiped her grandmother's eyes.

"Thank you Orchid. I can see clearly now. Your grandfather, Muhktar is standing in the corner holding a bouquet of flowers and waiting for me. He gave me flowers from the first day we met until the day before he died. Now he's here to assist me on my journey. You were always his favorite. You see he's smiling and nodding".

Orchid followed her grandmother's eyes but didn't see anyone. Her grandmother lifted a tiny, boney hand from beneath the covers and the pungent smell of raw ginger tingled her nostrils. Lifting the covers, Orchid looked at the pack of ginger wrapped in a sheer cloth between her grandmother's legs, and spread out across her groin, which Orchid knew was a remedy for pain.

"Where's Guzal?"

Orchid eased down the covers and again searched the corner for her grandfather. She thought of Auntie Guzal who she hadn't seen since her wedding but had heard from her mother that she'd taken a leave of absence from the clinic and had traveled somewhere the same day as Miriam and Ziyod had left for the United States at the end of the school year, a year and a half ago. Orchid had seen Ziyod loading luggage into Yusuf's brother's minivan taxi as soon as finals ended. Orchid had focused on Ziyod, causing him to turn in her direction, and seeing Orchid's look in his direction, had gotten into the van without looking back. Orchid had heard they were now living in California and were married.

"I'm here mama."

A sandpaper voice pulled Orchid's head around and she stifled the cry trying to escape from her mouth upon seeing the skeletal woman dressed in black with dark glasses standing in the doorway. Aunt Guzal's right hand shook and wobbling, she passed Orchid and walked around to the other side of her grandmother's bed, then bent and kissed her mother. Orchid's grandmother removed her other hand from beneath the covers and took her daughter's hand.

"I knew you'd come. I like your hair long like that. Russia has been good to you".

Aunt Guzal opened her purse and removed a silver ring with a quarter sized onyx stone sitting atop it, which she placed on her mother's third finger. The ring slid to the right on the thin finger.

"I brought you this ring mama. I know how much you love onyx".

The old woman kissed the ring and clenched Orchid's hand with her left hand, then placed Guzal's hand on top of Orchid's.

"I'm going to take my last breath in a few seconds but before I do, and join your father Guzal, and your grandfather Orchid, I want you two to promise you'll smooth the ruffled garment between you and talk. Promise me".

Orchid looked at her auntie through blurred eyes.

"I promise grandma."

"I promise mama".

The fading woman placed her hand on top of theirs.

"Now kiss, and remember what you've promised me."

Orchid leaned across her grandmother and met her aunt over her grandmother, then both women shared kisses on both cheeks. Orchid inhaled aunt Guzal's perfume and her cheekbone against Orchid's face. Auntie's glasses fell off and Orchid saw her aunt's hallowed, sunken, dark eyes. The grandmother eye's widened.

"Alright Hondamar. I'm ready".

Lifting her arms, she inhaled, closed her eyes and didn't exhale. Her body then shook. Auntie Guzal felt behind her mother's ear with her fingertips, then her jugular vein.

"Abdullahi. Please come. Mama's gone".

Abdullahi, Orchid's father, took slow steps into the room, then knelt beside the bed, placing his head on his mother's chest and wept loudly holding onto her hands. Orchid smelled lavender flowers and looked around the room for them. Her mother entered holding Orchid's nine-month old son, Umbir, who cried and clutched his grandmother's neck looking away from his great grandmother's body. Hearing his grandson's shrieking, Abdullahi Zaynitdinov stood and left the room. Auntie Guzal and Orchid kissed the now dead woman on both cheeks and hands clasped, walked from the room embracing each other's grief and closing behind them. Sitting in her living room, Auntie Guzal extended her arm, keeping Siroj, Orchid's husband from kissing her. She then rose, and entered her study with Orchid following.

"Auntie."

Auntie Guzal placed an open palm in Orchid's face. "I will make peace with you, but not with him Orchid. He's your husband, but he's a bad man and I'm going to show you. Now please excuse me. I have to call them to come and get mama".

Orchid left the room and dragged her bloated legs to the couch. Making sure a pillow was on the couch, she eased herself onto it. Her husband and father exited her aunt's house and she watched them standing outside, passing a tinted soda bottle which she knew contained alcohol. Orchid covered her face when the orderlies entered with the gurney and she heard the wheels moving, removing her grandmother from the house.

"Orchid, I'm going to ride with them to the clinic and perform the washing. I think I'll see you later".

Orchid dropped her hands and stared at her aunt whose head shook.

"Auntie, are you alright?"

Her aunt used a handkerchief to remove something which gurgled in her throat.

"No I'm not. I'm dying. I'm in the last stage of stage four cancer. I've been receiving treatment in Moscow over the last few months but there's no hope. We'll talk later. I know you're sad Orchid but try not to get to emotional. What you feel, your baby feels".

The bottom of her stomach turned sideways and her baby twisted inside her. Orchid rubbed the little knot protruding from her stomach and chuckled, thinking of her grandmother saying the baby was a girl because she calmed when Orchid rubbed the spot where the baby was. Her grandmother said the spot was the girl's butt and that women liked to be rubbed there.

Siroj, her husband, red eyed, too stepped into the room.

"Your aunt's very upset, and she looks awful. I guess Moscow wasn't good for her".

Red flashes of anger flashed in front of Orchid's eyes and the baby moved.

"How do you expect her to feel? Her mother and my grandmother just died".

Siroj lit a cigarette and blew the smoke into the air.

"She was very old and it's not like you all didn't expect her to die. And your aunt's angry at me and probably at herself for leaving".

Orchid tried to lift her legs onto the table to relieve the heaviness and to try and see her feet.

"She's not the only one angry at you so maybe it's justified".

Siroj glanced at Orchid's elephant sized feet and taking a drag from his cigarette, returned outside and getting the bottle from his father-in-law, emptied it. Orchid sucked her teeth watching him and her baby kicked. She'd been furious with Siroj since he mounted her three weeks after giving birth to their son and she got pregnant again. Orchid knew, he knew, she had no breast milk and could get pregnant because he was a doctor and had resented him, while loving her baby all during her pregnancy. Rubbing her moving baby again Orchid grunted trying to lift her feet and her mother, hearing her rushed from the bedroom and lifting her feet, placed a pillow under them.

"There you go. Didn't I just hear Siroj's voice in here?"

Orchid closed her eyes and pictured red tulips on the hillside, like a fiery carpet, which always calmed her, and was an experience she and Salim had shared because they'd once laid on the hillside together, and cuddling, shared the ecstasy the flowered image brought them.

"It's ok mother. I don't expect that from him".

"You should. He's your husband and you're carrying his child. He should be more considerate. Men".

She sat on the couch next to Orchid and taking Orchid's marshmallow puffed feet, began massaging them.

"I don't know why men are so blind. They only think about that thing between their legs and being powerful. What stupid creatures".

They both laughed and Orchid's mother wiggled her daughter's big toe, the way she'd done when Orchid was a little girl while singing the little piggy song. Her mother kissed Orchid's big toe.

"You know your aunt's dying don't you?"

The baby stirred.

"I know mother. She looks like a skeleton."

"Did you two make some peace? Orchid, if you didn't, you should before she dies. I can't tell you how I know, but I've always felt your aunt was wronged."

Orchid wiggled her toes.

"You never said that before mother".

Her mother placed Orchid's feet on the floor, retrieved her slip-on sandals, and grunting pulled Orchid to her feet. Water gushed from between Orchid's legs and splattered onto the floor. Orchid and her mother laughed, and her mother, rising and running, knocked on the window, signaled to her husband, and turned to Orchid.

"That was a big gush and we're far from the hospital. We'll have to go to Guzal's clinic".

She strode on her toes into the bedroom, dialed a number, throwing the receiver on the floor, and returned pushing a wheelchair. Orchid gritted her teeth in pain and clenched her buttocks together.

"Mommy, it's coming. I pooped myself."

Her mother pushed the wheelchair against Orchid's knees, making her sit down in the chair. Orchid frowned and wrinkled her nose, while her mother wheeled her out the door and down the ramp her father had built for his mother in law and Orchid. He helped her into the van.

"Life and death daughter. This is going to be a blessed child".

Orchid grabbed the back of the front seat and pushed away her husband's hand.

"Hurry papa. It's coming".

Abdullahi Zaynitdinov drove through the campus and stopped in front of the clinic. Auntie met them at the door in her electric wheelchair and followed them into the delivery room.

"Sit her on the table and slant it downward. I saw this African doctor do it in Moscow and it made delivery much easier".

Siroj reached for Orchid's arm.
"Get away from me Siroj. This is all your fault".
Siroj slunk back and left the room along with Orchid's father.
Orchid grunted and pushed as the table almost touched the floor and auntie reached down and lifted a screaming long haired big girl. Orchid extended her arms.

"Give her to me. Give her to me. Give her to me".

Auntie cut the umbilical cord and handed the big baby to Orchid. The child ceased to cry, and Orchid kissed her forehead.

"She looks like grandma".

Her aunt finished cleaning up Orchid.

"That she does. How ironic".

....

Orchid held her baby daughter, Mehruz, with misty eyes marveling at the stream of milk gushing from her breast. Siroj stood over her, gazing down at his daughter, but as he reached for her, Orchid pulled away. Her mother and father focused on Umbir's crimson face, but all their attention turned to the door, hearing auntie's chair.

"I think we should go ahead and say goodbye to mama now, instead of some public demonstration. Abdullahi help Orchid into the wheelchair and bring her back here."

Orchid rolled out of bed on her own and sat in the wheelchair with her new baby girl. Her mother carried little Umbir, and Siroj tagged along behind her father pushing the wheelchair. They entered a cool back room with an open casket containing the matriarch dressed in black and other family members filled the room. Auntie opened her arms to Abdullahi Zaynitdinov, her brother, who stood in front of his mother's casket.

"My mother was a kind woman who loved orange spice tea and cooking. She cooked a special plate for my sister and I, and when our father died when she was only 40, like a good Muslim woman she never married again. She was a good grandmother to all her grandchildren and lived a full life".

Biting his lip, he returned and stood behind Orchid while the other family members spoke kindly of his mother. The family then left with Siroj, Orchid's father and Farid, wheeling out the casket which carried her grandmother's body, leaving Orchid and her auntie alone.

Auntie's head bobbed as she sat by Rose's bed.

"Auntie, are you alright?"

"No, I'm not alright, I'm dying, and I'm angry because it's taking too long. I want it to be over Orchid. This pain is unnecessary and my old body wants to rest".

Orchid rocked her child and watched her aunt's hands opening and closing.

"God has his own time schedule auntie".

Auntie Guzal looked.

"Well mister. I think I'm going to punch my own clock and meet you on my own time."

Orchid raised her head upward.

"He probably hears you and is as confused as I am auntie".

Her aunt threw a kiss in the air, then opened her purse sitting in a pouch on the side of her chair. She drove her chair close to Orchid's bed and parked it.

"Take this envelope and don't open it until two weeks after my death niece. Promise me the way you promised mama we'd talk".

Orchid took the 8 ½ by 11 envelop and kissed her auntie's hands.

"I promise auntie. Can we speak honestly now?"

Her aunt drove to the door, closed it and returned to Orchid's bed. She patted Orchid's foot and raised her hand in the air.

"I swear on everything sacred to me and on my mother's life which just left us I didn't sleep with Salim, your fiancé. Is that what you want to know?"

Orchid peered into her aunt's electric flashing eyes.

"Yes auntie. That's what I wanted to ask you. But the photographs?"

Auntie rubbed her deep sunken eyes.

"It's 2001 and anything can be done. Just open the envelope in two weeks. I want to talk some more but I'm exhausted Orchid. I love you and you've always been the daughter I never had. Take care of yourself".

Her arms trembling as she raised herself from the wheelchair, she kissed Orchid, eased herself back into her chair and turning around, her head falling to one side, drove to the door.

"Mehran, I need your help getting into the bed and putting in a morphine drip".

Orchid heard her aunt's chair motor fading down the hallway and saw Mehran, her assistant trotting behind her. The baby made a sound so Orchid moved the cradle beside her bed, then closed her eyes to rest.

She was awakened by the baby crying, and a blue light flashing. Lifting Mehruz, she glimpsed her mother's back running from her room.

Rocking Mehruz, she smoothed down the thick black hair and returned the baby's smile.

Her mother, handkerchief to her mouth entered the room and wiped the bars from her face.

"Auntie is gone Orchid."

Orchid placed Mehruz in her bassinette. A wave of sadness, starting at the top of her

skull, dribbled down through her and stopped at her eyes.

"She was just here some hours ago".

"It was soon because she took her own life Orchid. She gave herself too much medicine and she overdosed. She knew what she was doing. I hope God doesn't punish her. The Koran says suicide is a sin".

Orchid remembered her aunt's words.

"I think God will understand mother because she was in a lot of pain and couldn't stand it anymore. God is merciful and benevolent. I'm just glad auntie is free, though I'm sad. Mother, I need to sleep. This is too much for one day".

Turning towards Mehruz, she closed her eyes and drifted away.

CHAPTER NINE

Two weeks later Orchid, Umbir her son, Mehruz
and her mother sat in her living room, which before
had been her aunt's. Aunt Guzal had left Orchid her
house, car, jewelry, all her possessions, and all the
money in her bank accounts, along with a note
saying "you can now buy your own bread and
spread your wings". The note and all the accounts
was in an envelope inside the envelop her aunt had
asked her to open in two weeks and it was now
time. Her husband was at the hospital, and her
father at work. Orchid fingered the same size
envelope, inside the other envelope and opened it.
She first looked at receipt from a Moscow
photography studio, then looked at the signature. It
was signed by Siroj, her husband. She then read an
account ledger from the same studio, with the

account holder being her father. Showing the ledger to her mother, Orchid's breath came in short bursts and the top of her skull tingled. Her mother inhaled and exhaled.

"Oh my God. No Orchid. No!"

Orchid emptied the contents onto the living room table, picked up another piece of paper, which she and her mother read together. It was an order form for reconstructed photographs. Taking the photographs from the table, they saw her aunt's picture, Salim's picture, different sex scenes with a black and white couple, then the final results which were Salim and her aunt's faces on the couple's bodies. Her mother jumped to her feet and ran to the downstairs bathroom. Orchid could hear her vomiting, and stones filled her lungs. Her mother returned to the living room and they wrapped up the children and drove to her father's office, her mother repeating his name. Carrying the children, they entered his office and found him looking out the window. Turning around, Orchid threw the pictures on his desk. Abdullahi Zaynitdinov spread the pictures with open hands, raised his eyes to Orchid and her mother, then collapsed on the floor, his eyes showing only the whites, his right arm shaking, and blood coming from his left ear.

Orchid sat in an "s" position, wearing a full length pea coat Salim had bought for her, which was glued to her body, trying to melt the glacier residing in her bones, and holding her mother's ice cube hand, in the hospital emergency room. Her father had been rushed into surgery immediately and she watched the operating room door while her mother prayed, her mouth moving without sound. The clacking sound of heels on tile drew their attention and turning they saw Farid's ashen face and long lean figure striding across the room towards them.

Squatting in front of their mother, then taking her hands and kissing them, he smoothed a tear away with the Venus palm of his hand.

"Don't worry mother. God will protect him".

Their mother clasped his hand with both of hers and held it as Farid stood over Orchid.

"If he dies, it's your fault and you'll carry his death to your grave. You can never leave anything alone."

Orchid returned the narrow venom look Farid shot at her.

"I did nothing but confront him with what he'd done to my life. It was his guilt which harmed him, not me. And if you had a conscience you'd probably feel something but you don't because you have no shame. You, he and Siroj who were all part of this.

How dare you blame me? Blame yourselves for twisting my life into something you could control".

Farid pointed a long first finger at Orchid.

"What would our lives have been if you'd have married that American? Tell me Orchid. What family would have accepted me and Gulnora with that marriage? Huh? We would have ended up with someone beneath us because of the shame you'd have brought on our family. Think about someone other than yourself".

Orchid slapped Farid's finger from her face and standing, their noses touched and she smelled the whisky he'd been drinking.

"No you think of someone other than yourself Farid. You're bending your assistant over her desk every day trying to hump away your unhappiness. And Gulnora is so unhappy that she tries to eat hers away. I put the family first and look at what's come from it".

Farid rocked on his heels and moved backwards.

"You have two beautiful children Orchid. As does Gulnora and myself, and our family's where it should be. Isn't that enough?"

Orchid grabbed Farid in the collar.

"No it's not because it's all built on a lie".

Farid twisted Orchid's wrist, forcing her to release him, and plopped into the chair next to his praying mother.

"Well it is for me".

The operating room's doors opened and Siroj approached them carrying his white operating room cap.

"Thank God he's going to be fine. He's had a stroke. There's partial paralysis in the right arm, but he'll eventually gain use of it. However, he's lost his ability to speak, and we have no idea if that will ever return. It's doubtful".

He reached for Orchid who swiped at his hand.

"Don't touch me Siroj"

Her mother eased herself into the chair behind her and raised both arms.

"Thank you Allah!"

Farid and Siroj took her hands and they prayed together. Orchid, arms crossed, bit the skin inside her mouth, waited until they'd stopped, then pulled Siroj away from her mother and brother. Siroj kept his eyes on Orchid's hand until she released his arm.

"Orchid, it's not the time for whatever you want to fight about. Your father's very sick".

Orchid's neck burned.

"I know he's sick and it's more than the stroke. You and he tricked me into marrying you. That's the real sickness you and he have".

She took each picture, touched his forehead with them, and watched the color fade from his face.

"Your father made me do that Orchid. If I hadn't, he wouldn't have let me marry you".

Orchid placed her body against Siroj's and placed her mouth to his ear.

"Well you did, we have children, and I hope you enjoy feeling my body against yours because it's the last feel you'll ever get. Understand this Siroj. I hate you and I'll never sleep with you again. You can be a father to my children, but you'll never have a wife. Not me at least".

Turning, she helped Farid lift her mother from the chair and they walked to her father's room.

BOOK THREE

CHAPTER TEN

Orchid, Gulnora, Iroda, Orchid's cousin and her sister Muhktasar lounged in Orchid's television room, watching their children rolling and crawling across the carpet. Umbir, her son was 3, Mehruz, her daughter 2, Iroda's son Sobir 3 and Gulnora's son Dilshod was 1. The women watched as the boys threw their trucks and soldiers across the room and the girls played with their toys. Iroda raised her chin towards her son.

"Look he's violent like his father."

Orchid grinned, seeing Umbir having his action figures fighting.

"All males are like that. It's their nature. Even as men they never grow out of it."

Gulnora raised her hand for a five.

"That's why none of us have one."

The women exchanged fives then settled into the valley of their aloneness. All were divorced, except Orchid, who had filed for divorce but Siroj still refused to sign the papers. She saw him almost every day because he walked across the campus on his way to the hospital, now being the head of the anesthesiology department, and to pick up the children to take them to daycare. He also visited her father every day and they walked together, her father scribbling notes to Siroj because his ability to speak had never returned. Farid, who'd taken her father's position as head of the college also walked with them and the three men, along with Umbir attended boxing and soccer matches weekly.

Orchid and the women heard the front door open, her mother's voice, then stopped upon hearing a man's voice. Her sister and cousins, also hearing the man's voice, covered themselves with wraps because they'd been lounging in shorts or sheer garments. Orchid asked her mother who'd she brought and a familiar voice called her name. Pausing to recognize the voice Orchid scuttled from the room and jumped into the man's arms.

"Ziyod. Oh God it's been so long. You look amazing".

She admired his grey silk suit, grey shoes, white silk collarless shirt with a black diamond in the center, with grey socks and shoes. Ziyod's chest stuck out.

"I went to the English department but they said you'd taken the day off so I went to your parents' house and your mother brought me here. How are you dear Orchid?"

Typical Ziyod she thought to herself. Asking peering questions and expecting insightful answers.

"I'm well Ziyod. I love the teaching and I'm now head of the department after only three years".

Ziyod stretched his neck and dove into Orchid's eyes.

"That wasn't my question".

Orchid looked over her shoulder towards the TV room, listening for her mother's voice with the children.

"I live here with my sister and her children. And Siroj is gone from my life because I discovered the truth. And I never loved him. Ziyod, thank you for visiting me. I"

Ziyod pressed his piano fingers to her lips.

"We all make mistakes Orchid, and you made a grand one. And life is too short to worry about the past. I'm a father now. My son Salim is two, very tall and he's already at the piano".

Opening his wallet, he showed her a recent photograph of he, Miriam and his son. The wallet slipped and catching it, the photographs flipped over and she saw Salim, holding his trumpet in a photograph. The blood from her heart, filled her eyes and she held the picture, moving her fingers over Salim's face.

"He's still single Orchid".
Orchid handed Ziyod his wallet and melted into her sofa.
"Do they still hate me?"
Ziyod sat at the far end of the sofa, packed his pipe and lit it.

"They never did. They're not like us. We hold grudges and are vindictive. They must be the most forgiving people I've ever met. Honestly, Orchid, they felt sorry for you. Especially when Shahknoza told them what you discovered."

Orchid used her hand like scissors.

"Shahknoza's tongue."

"You couldn't have a better friend Orchid. She told us because she knows where your heart is".

Orchid placed both hands over her heart. Then sat up, hearing a knock at the door. Opening it, she and Gulnora's mother in law burst into the room.

"Where is she?"

Orchid stepped in front of her.

"My sister lives here now and she's in another room. Why?"

The mother in law adjusted her expensive spring jacket and Louis Vuitton purse.

"I know she lives here but she must return to the house with my grandson. I won't lose another."

Orchid lowered her head. She knew Gulnora didn't want to return to that house because she had lived there with the woman they called "Ticky", because she was so particular about everything. She followed Orchid when she lived there, and Gulnora around the house watching what they did and constantly telling them how to fold sheets, place forks in a drawer, spoons in the drawer, how to wash clothes, iron, hang up her own clothes, smelled and tasted the food they made while they were cooking, adding spices Orchid and Gulnora didn't like, saying it was what their husbands enjoyed, and even watching as they brushed their teeth, telling them they were pushing too hard and not making wide enough circles on their teeth. Orchid had decided she was living in a prison, and hives developed across her back and when she complained to Siroj, he responded by telling her she was in his mother's house and if she wanted to be a good wife, to learn what his mother liked and how she wanted everything in order to get along. Orchid had spent her days in her mother's home, only returning at night to sleep, after dinner, and had fought her mother-in-law by denying her access to Umbir, who cried whenever his grandmother picked him up. Gulnora had learned to do the same and they'd danced in a circle when Orchid had inherited her aunt's house, and before when Orchid had moved in to take care of her grandmother.

"Respectfully mother, if you had raised sons who weren't dishonest and in Gulnora's case violent, you'd have access to your grandchild all the time".

The mother-in-law flipped her hair and spinning around, left Orchid's house. Ziyod stirred his pipe.

"You have become very vocal. It's good".

They discussed Ziyod's having returned to Tashkent to have the remainder of his belongings shipped to the U.S. where he'd accepted a university position, and Miriam, now in her residency and Ziyod's new body which came from regular workouts with Salim. Orchid knew, Ziyod saw, that mentioning Salim cracked her reservoir of sadness a bit more and that her chest fluttered, but he didn't continue any conversation about Salim.

Finishing his bowl, Ziyod, emptied his pipe into a leather pouch and stood.

"There's something called Skype Orchid, and people can see anyone they're conversing with. Salim is on there. You might try and find him. I have to be at the airport in an hour. Farewell, dear Orchid. If you ever make it to California, look us up. You'll be more than welcome".

Kissing Orchid, Ziyod handed her a card and left her home. Turning the card over she read, Dr. Salim Akbar, surgeon, UCLA medical center, Beverly Hills, California. The card also contained Salim's phone number, email address, cell phone and his pager. Orchid returned to her couch, then getting her telephone, called Salim's cell number. It rang five times, and upon hearing his sleepy voice, she hung up, and wept into the pillow she used to cover her face.

Walking to the television room, Orchid passed the children's room and paused to observe her mother on the floor, on cushions, asleep holding the one-year-old, with the other children asleep snuggled next to her.

She continued to the television room, where her sister and cousins sat, watching a movie about a student who fell in love with her professor, and they were separated because of the situation, then found each other after some years and were together for life. Orchid watched the movie with them, then moaning, emptied her heart into another pillow. Soon all the women shared their aloneness into pillows, scarves, hands, and Orchid prepared each a bowl from Ziyod's father's supply, which she now had, and they smoked and laughed and fell asleep in the television room together.

6 a.m. the next morning, Orchid sat in front of her computer and typed in a friend request to akbarmdtrumpet on skype. Wiping both palms on a towel, she waited for a response and received an acceptance. Orchid clapped her hands, then rising to leave heard someone clear their voice and turned to see Salim sitting behind a desk in a white doctor's coat. Sitting down, and clad in only her red nightie, she listened to the song by Milestone, I Care about

You, then Tevin Campbell's Can We Talk. Salim

blew Orchid a kiss, and clearing his throat again,

adjusted the camera, showing a picture of them

laying in a field of red tulips in the mountains

outside Tashkent.

"Hey Orchid!"

Bubbles formed in Orchid's eyes.

"Hey Salim, salami!"

His dark eyes glimmered, he placed both huge

hands against the side of his face, and the screen

went black. They'd lost the connection and after ten

attempts, Orchid returned to her bedroom, crawled

into her bed, and taking out a white collarless shirt

she'd kept of his, smelled it, then put it on, the

sleeves hanging past her hands, and placing the

bottom part between her thighs, she touched herself,

exploring deep avenues inside where she thought he

would touch and called out his name until she

reached the peak of her mountain and her lava exploded through the sheet and onto the mattress. Hearing Guzal's baby crying, awakened her from the ecstasy which enthralled her, and opening her door, Gulnora, Iroda, Mukhtasar and Orchid's mother stood outside her room. Orchid looked at the floor while turning to go back into her room and Gulnora, and her cousins laughed, all pinching Orchid on the bottom. Closing the door her mother knocked.

"Is Salim still in there?"

Orchid placed a folded towel over her soaked bottom sheet, pulled the top sheet over the towel and reclining on her back, kept Salim's shirt to her nose, tucking it between her legs again and fastening the bottom button so that it would stay close to her thighs, and rubbed her nipples in a twelve o'clock position. She pulled up the covers as the bedroom door opened and Gulnora entered.

"What were you doing?"

Orchid sniffed the shirt.

"I guess I was dreaming?"

Gulnora pulled down the covers.

"Dreaming. Hmph. I'm your sister and you can't lie to me because I know you. What were you doing?"

Orchid lifted the shirt and blew on her nipples.

"I was with Salim and just touching myself"

Gulnora lay next to her on the bed.

"Where and how do you do it? I wasn't close to auntie like you and as you know, mother never talked to us... Did Salim touch you?"

Orchid covered her face with the shirt again and giggled as she bobbed her head affirmatively.

Lowering the cover, she wiggled her tongue.

Gulnora sat up on her knees.

"You're kidding. Down here? Hondamar has never done that. He's like Umbir and Iroda's husband Fuad. It's almost always fast and only for himself. I have to hold him there to ever get pleased."

Raising her hands, the two sister's slapped fives.

"They're the three-minute family."

Iroda opened the door and entered the room.

"I heard that. You're talking about our husbands".

Orchid told Iroda and Gulnora to get three mirrors, which they did and placing them on the floor, the women disrobed and squatted, and Orchid showed them how to find their G spot, then about Salim, and what, where, and how he'd touched her. She then told them where she touched herself, about seeing Salim on Skype, then held her sister and cousin who both cried.

CHAPTER ELEVEN

Orchid sat in her office as dean of the English department at the University of diplomacy observing her father, his steps slow and deliberate, a five-pound weight in his right hand, Umbir on his back in a child's holster, Mohammad, Siroj's father, Siroj, and Farid take their daily walk across the green and around the campus. Her father, unable to speak, moved his head and his free left hand and occasionally adjusted Umbir on his back, her son's long legs touching his grandfather's waist. He had his grandfather's domed head, forehead, but her almond shaped eyes, full mouth and his father's long thin legs. She knew they would pass the International corner as everyone called it. The corner Salim had established, where Uzbek students bought and exchanged international music, mostly from the U.S. Salim never took money, like the others, and only exchanged Uzbek articles for the music he exchanged, sending the artifacts home. Her son's hands and feet though were thick, wide and long like her mother. Mehruz, her baby girl pulled herself onto Orchid's lap and ran the tips of her thick baby fingers under Orchid's chin, sucking her thumb. She liked to do that and place her fat head between Orchid's breast. What a chunk she was at birth, and they'd had to stitch Orchid up because Mehruz had been so big. Orchid and her aunt said she looked like a two-month old hairy baby, with her short pudgy legs and doughy body. Orchid loved her, but looking at her, she saw her mother in law, and the child even had her temperament, crying a lot as an infant, and trying to fight her brother all the time. She was fussy, stubborn, and would dominate other children if they couldn't defend themselves. Orchid had to be firm with her, and she'd squint up her face, her mouth like a bulldog when she didn't want to do something. Orchid rubbed her chin on her daughter's bushy curls and was startled when hearing one ring from Skype, then Salim's face. He wore a red body shirt and she seeing bulges under it crossed her legs, squeezing the tingling moving through her under garments.

"Is that your baby girl?"

He spoke to Mehruz in Uzbek and smiling she opened and closed her hand at him. Salim took pencils, putting one in each nostril, another two in both sides of his mouth, held one in each hand behind his head and grunting, moved his head from side to side. Mehruz squealed with delight and wiggled in Orchid's lap.

"You know how to make children laugh Salaami. Me too."

Face flushed, she held his gaze and placed an open palm on the computer's screen.

"Salim. I'm sorry and so ashamed that I want to crawl under a rock and hide for being so stupid. It's hard for me to face you Salim. How could I ever think you'd do something like that when it's not your personality?"

Salim's hand almost covered the screen.

"Shhhhh. It's alright my sweet flower. Those we love can hurt us the most because we don't expect them to do anything harmful. Your father loves you Orchid. He and Siroj."

Mehruz climbed on Orchid's desk and placed a pudgy hand on the scream.

"Hello Mr. Animal!"

Her squeaky child's voice moved them both to laughter. Salim removed his hand.

"I called to congratulate you."

Orchid helped Mehruz to the floor.

"For what?"

Salim ran his tongue over his teeth. Orchid knew he did this when puzzled by something.

"Have you opened your mail today?"

Orchid picked up the letters on her desk and tore open the letter from the American Embassy in Tashkent. Reading the letter, she jumped into the air screaming, causing Mehruz to fall and bump her head against the chair leg. She puckered her mouth but didn't cry. Orchid's secretary opened the door and Orchid turned the computer screen away from her.

"I just won the visa lottery to go to the United States. I just won the visa lottery to go to the United States."

The secretary shrugged and closed the door. Orchid sat in her chair and spun the monitor around.

"How'd you know? Salim, did you have something to do with this?"

Salim pounded his chest like a gorilla.

"Yes, and no. I know the ambassador, and I did speak to her. There's a catch though. Read the letter carefully".

Orchid read the letter again and placed it on her desk.

"It says Mr. and Mrs. And therefore he can come too. My not being divorced has come back to haunt me".

Salim's thumping his chin signaled yes and that he was concerned. Orchid helped Mehruz into her lap and watched the four men walking towards her parent's house.

"I'll deal with that the best way I can, Salim. Right now I'm just happy I'll be near you again and we can at least talk".

Both Orchid and Salim placed open palms against the computer screen and Mehruz joined them.

BOOK FOUR

CHAPTER TWELVE

Orchid, Siroj, Umbir, and Mehruz sat in her father's
house with her parents, Gulnora and her husband,
Iroda and her husband, Farid, his pregnant wife
Nazifa, and Siroj's parents. Gulnora and Iroda's
husbands were Siroj's brothers and Nazifa was his
sister. They all stood while Farid read a blessing
written by their father, everyone prayed together,
exchanged eye dripping kisses, hugs, and gifts.
Orchid's mother and father ushered Orchid into
another room. Her mother sopping up the flow from
her eyes handed Orchid a note.

"I said this to you before when you graduated, and when you got married. You can now buy your own bread and though my methods were questionable and I hurt you, daughter, you can do it. You're going to America and you already have a job, which shows I was right in that way, but I was wrong in other ways. Completely wrong. Go with strength and the love in my heart for you, Orchid".

Covering his face, he wept loudly on his wife's chest and Orchid went to her knees and kissed his and her mother's feet, thanking them for giving her life. Rising, she walked backwards through her family, an anvil sitting on her neck, and entered Yusuf's brother's taxi.

"I'll call you as I arrive and I'll see you all in three months when you come visit me".

Comforting her children plastered under her arms, she glanced at the Tashkent sky, and allowed the door to be closed. Opening the taxi window, she watched the stars skating across the Taskent sky and shouted I love you and I'll miss you to Uzbekistan.

An hour later, sitting in the Tashkent airport lounge and waiting to board the Aeroflot Russian airplane. Siroj looked down at his children on both sides of Orchid.

"Thank you for this opportunity. I know it wasn't easy for you".

Orchid rubbed her chin on top of Mehruz's head and the little girl tickled her mother's side.

"I didn't have a choice. It said Mr. and Mrs. and I didn't want to lose this opportunity, so you don't have to thank me, Siroj".

She watched the board for the flight and the stewards attending at the announcement desk. Siroj handed her an envelope.

"Open it and read it."

Orchid looked at the heading on the envelop which said AMA, American Medical Association. Curious, she opened the envelope and read the letter stating Siroj had passed the medical association exam and could work in the U.S. She flipped the envelope to Siroj and he caught it.

"How'd you do it Siroj? Your English isn't good enough to pass that exam."

Siroj leaned back in his chair, an alligator grin beaming.

"We all have our sources and mine are substantial". Orchid face burned.

"I hope you studied instead of cheating like you did to pass this test. You won't be sitting in an office in a U.S. hospital. You'll have to work and you'll have people's lives in your hands".

Siroj grit his teeth.

"I sat at a desk because my father worked for it just like yours did to help you and Farid sit at desks. And I'm as competent as the next doctor in what I do".

The airlines announced first class boarding and Siroj rose and got in the line. Orchid observed Umbir and Mehruz's heads turned towards their father standing in line.

"Come on children. It's time to go to America".

CHAPTER THIRTEEN

Orchid waited for Siroj and the porter to bring their luggage outside LAX airport. She had seen Shahknoza circle the airport highway in a Mercedes SUV, waving and shouting her name and she'd thumbed her nose at Shahknoza to let her know she'd seen her. Siroj and the porter arrived just as the SUV pulled to the curb and Shaknoza jumped from the SUV.

"Orchid. Oh my god. I didn't think you'd make it. I've been waiting for this day for years and I'm very glad you're here. My, look at this little boy. He looks just like you and he's going to be tall just like his uncle and look at his head, Orchid. It's just like your father's. And where did you get this munchkin from? She'd got chair legs and a fat round bottom and she looks like. Oh my God Orchid, she looks like your mother-in-law. Oh my God. Oh my God. Oh my God. She marked her. Get in the car with them. Hello Siroj. Welcome to America".

They all entered the SUV and the children immediately fell asleep. Siroj stared out the window. Where's Yusuf?"

Shahknoza watched the road.

"He has an away game in Kansas City and will return tomorrow".

Siroj leaned towards Shahknoza and she leaned back.

"I didn't know he was now playing in Los Angeles?"

Shahknoza stared ahead.

"There's a lot you don't know".

She nudged Orchid who swallowed her smile.

They drove through traffic to a place called Hidden Hills and Orchid, carrying Mehruz followed Shahknoza into the three story house followed by Siroj, carrying Umbir. Orchid rubber necked looking around her new house.

"It looks bigger inside than online."

Shahknoza smacked Orchid on the bottom.

"Of course silly. It's a computer. Siroj, give me the boy. I'll carry him upstairs. You can have a drink in the den. It's down the hall, near another bedroom".

Siroj's neck stiffened.

"I'll carry my son to his room".

Shahknoz sucked her teeth and led them upstairs, passing the master bedroom, upstairs lounge room, other bedrooms and finally to the children's bedrooms.

"See Orchid, they're just like you wanted them".

Orchid placed Mehruz in her red bed, the color she liked and after removing the child's clothes, walked through the adjoining door and waited while Siroj undressed Umbir and put him in the bed. He walked into the bathroom in the bedroom and looked at the soccer players' posters on the wall.

"I see you have all the players he likes".

Orchid took Shahknoza's hand.

"It's his room and I know what he likes".

Leaving Siroj in the room, the two women went downstairs and into the kitchen. Orchid ran her hand over the island in the middle with the room.

"Thank you Shahknoz for finding me this house. I don't know what I would have done without you.

Shahknoz spun around in the room.

"I know. And what are you going to do about him?"

Orchid took Shahknoz's hand again and walked down the hall to the back door, opened it, and pointed to the guest house in the backyard about thirty feet from the house and away from the pool.

"He'll live there until he finds his own place. He had someone take the medical exam for him so he can work here. I'll just have to wait".

Shahknoza peered over her shoulder.

"I know, but he won't have to look very hard. Salim found him a job at Cedar's Sinai Hospital where he works. He'll start Monday. That will give him a few days to get over jet lag".

Orchid hugged Shahknoza and also glanced over her shoulder.

"But won't he find out?"

Shahknoza wiggled her head.

"No, because he'll think Yusuf helped him. We worked it out. Now let's go inside".

Entering the house Siroj was coming down the stairs. He passed them and went into the den, then closed the door. Orchid heard him open a cabinet, take a glass and pour, what she knew was Vodka. Shahknoza patted her bottom and blew an open palm towards the den.

"There's enough liquor in there to keep him for awhile. I'm worried though Orchid about how he's going to react when you show him where he'll be living".

Orchid sat at the table in the kitchen nook.

"He lives in his mother's house in Tashkent, Shahknoz, and not with us. He and his brothers. Living in America will be no different".

Shahknoza stayed for a couple of hours, then rose to leave. Orchid accompanied her to the door and Shahknoz faced Orchid before she walked to the waiting car.

'Lock your door tonight".

Orchid pushed Shahknoz outside.

'You're so crazy. I told you that you should be a writer because your imagination is always running wild. I know him and he won't do anything. What time will you be here tomorrow?"

Shahknoz pinched Orchid's nose.

"Around ten. Then we'll go to the consulate so that you can meet your new colleagues".

Orchid watched Shahknoza enter the car and leave, then went to the den and knocked on the door. Siroj, drink in hand opened it.

"Come Siroj, I'll show you your house".

Siroj downed his drink and followed Orchid outside, past the pool, to the guest house. Giving him the keys she stepped away from the door.

"This is where you'll live until you find your own place".

Siroj opened the door and went inside the two-story guest house.

"I guess you saw this when you bought this place and you furnished it?"

Orchid moved further away from the door.

"Yes, I did and I tried to make it as comfortable for you as I can".

Siroj came to the door, started to close it, then opened the door wide.

"I guess my bags have been brought in."

Orchid curtsied.

"Yes, they have and we have someone who'll clean your house for you".

Siroj turned and went to the bar in the sunken living room and poured himself a straight vodka.

"Close the door, Orchid".

Orchid went to her bedroom and turned on the Skype. It was 9 p.m. in Los Angeles and 9 a.m. in Tashkent. Gulnora, her mom and dad sat at the computer and they discussed her house and Shahknoza, then hung up with the promise of a conversation after Orchid's first day at her new job as assistant director at the Uzbekistan consulate. After ending the conversation, Orchid went into her private shower, sat in the steam for awhile, then let the jet streams sooth her aching body and wash off the 15-hour plane ride. She then slipped into Salim's shirt and climbed into her bed, his shirt to her nose, his scent filling her, and pressed her pelvis

271

against the bottom sheet, feeling the firmness cushion the throbbing of her button. She'd fallen asleep, thinking of the dime sized curls of hair on Salim's stomach, and him lifting her in the air, when she thought she heard a trumpet blast then someone pushing her face into the pillow and ripping his shirt off her.

"You're still my wife and I won't let you treat me less than a man. And since you do, I'm going to mount you like a male dog mounts his bitch and treat you like the bitch you are".

Orchid heard seven one note trumpet notes and raised her hands.

"You're right Siroj. I am still your wife, and if you're going to go in the back, at least let me raise up on my knees and spread so it won't hurt me so much. There's even some lotion there you can put inside so that it will ease the pain. I'll lie here while you get it."

She felt Siroj push her face more into the pillow, heard him squish the lotion from the bottle and felt the cool lotion applied to her rectum. She raised her head enough again to speak.

"Now let me get on my knees so that you can take me".

Siroj removed his hand from her neck, and Orchid lifted her body then kicked backwards with all her power to Siroj's solar plexus which was step one in the seven step defense maneuver. She heard him grunt, then swung back her right elbow to his left temple. Step two, left elbow to right temple. Step three, roll his body off with her legs. Step four, fist between the eyes. Step five, grab something to subdue and wrap. Step six, and seven, another blow and call the police, which she didn't do. Siroj's eyes rolled in his head and he jerked, gasping for air, then closed his eyes, unconscious.

"You did everything right except steps six seven and I know you didn't because he's your children's father and you don't want to begin his life here by sending him to jail."

Orchid looked at the computer screen and saw Salim, holding his trumpet.

"I saw him before you did and that's why I blew my horn. He stood there watching you move on the bed before he attacked you. Dear Orchid, please turn off the eye on your computer in the future".

Orchid stared at the unconscious Siroj on the floor, Salim's shirt ripped in half, then looking down at her nakedness, put on the two shirt halves and covered herself.

"Thank you Salim. I never thought he'd…

Salim rubbed his lips.

"It's ok. Shahknoza has that special gift and she sensed something. You should listen to her".

The doorbell rang twice and Orchid went to the buzzer which had a camera and flicked it on. Iskander, Siroj's cousin stood at the door. Orchid pushed the microphone.

"What is it Iskander?"

Iskander extinguished his cigarette.

"Siroj called me to come and get him and to wait outside. Tell him I'm here. I'll wait outside".

Orchid's attention turned to Siroj's raspy voice. "Untie me Orchid. I'll go and never return again".

Orchid pushed the microphone again.

"He'll be right down".

Taking a letter opener from her drawer for protection, she untied Siroj's hands and feet, and watched him crawl across the floor, out of the room, then stumble down the steps and open the door. She heard Iskander's voice.

"What happened to you?"

Siroj eeked out an answer.

"I'm drunk and I fell down the stairs in the dark. Put my suitcases in the car and let's go".

Orchid watched Siroj stagger to Iskander's Mercedes from the monitor, then saw Iskander look into the camera and give her his middle finger. Turning off the camera, she sat in front of the computer and adjusted the eye so that the camera was only on her face.

"Are you alright Orchid?"

Salim blew smoke into the air.

"Yes, I'm alright. Just a bit shaken"

He fingered the trumpet's valves.

"Shall I come over?"

Orchid blew him a kiss.

"No, not tonight. I'll probably see you tomorrow, and if not, then soon. Ok?"

Salim played the first bar of Dedicated To You. Orchid knew the words. "If I could write, a tune for you. That brought me fame, and fortune too. That song would be, like my heart and me. Dedicated to you".

Blowing Salim a kiss, she reached for the off switch on the computer.

"Orchid, lock the doors. You can do it from the panel in your room".

Orchid turned off the computer, hit the house lock button, and climbed into bed, warmed by Salim's torn shirt.

The phone ringing, along with the house buzzer awakened Orchid, and her two children plastered to her sides. Reaching for the phone, Umbir, who always slept on her left side, opened his midnight dark eyes. Orchid kissed his forehead.

"Happy fifth birthday!"

She placed the phone to her ear and heard Shahknoza squawking about how long she'd been at the door and that it was 4:30 in the afternoon. Orchid rose from the bed, pushed the buzzer allowing the door to open and signaled for Umbir to go to his room, then lifting Mehruz, went into her bathroom. Shahknoz came into her room and stopped seeing Orchid in the bathroom.

"Give her to me. I'll give her a bath while you get ready. Don't worry about your meetings. I cancelled them. What happened to Salim's shirt?"

Orchid rubbed her eyes.

"Siroj, just like you said".

Shahknoza carried Mehruz from the room, giving Orchid a look from over her shoulder.

"You still don't know men."

Showering and dressing, she wondered to herself if Shahknoz was correct. Siroj had been understanding and accepting of her anger and distrust in Tashkent, and had never tried to even touch her. But a scene remained in her mind's eye of being children, and Siroj being angry with a boy who'd bullied him, and waiting until he had the boy in his house, then throwing boiling water in the boy's face. He was vindictive like that. She also recalled he had a surgeon from the hospital whom he saw regularly, whom she knew had won the visa lottery to the States a year before Orchid had, and had immigrated to the U.S.

Umbir entered her bedroom dressed in sky blue, his favorite color.

"Mommy, I want to grow my hair longer. I'm five now and I think it's time I wear my hair the way I want. Are we going to school now, or after we eat?"

Orchid's heart fluttered at his proclamation, and she noticed how his chest was full of air. Males were nothing like females. Mehruz already brushed her hair the way she wanted, without saying a word, but he had to rear up like a rooster.

"If that's what you want son. We can't go to school today because it's four o'clock in the afternoon".

Umbir looked at his watch. It was a gift his grandfather had given him before he left Tashkent. Orchid watched his eyes widen.

"Oh mommy, we slept all day".

Orchid embraced her son. She could smell the shampoo in his hair and made a mental note to rinse it again when she had time.

"It's called jet lag. Our bodies have to adjust to being in this time zone. I guess your watch adjusted automatically. Give me a minute and I'll prepare you something special for your birthday."

Shahknoza entered the room with Mehruz dressed in red.

"That won't be necessary because we're going out to dinner."

Both children clapped their hands. Walking down the stairs, Orchid noticed an 8 ½ x 11 envelope on the counter. Opening it and looking inside, she saw that Siroj had signed the divorce papers in the U.S. Showing them to Shahknoz, Umbir's squeal, and his holding a wooden box, drew their attention. He opened the box and inside was a note saying go to my house outside. Orchid and Shahknoza followed the running children who ran into the open house. Umbir jumped into the air upon seeing a new guitar sitting on a guitar stand with packs of strings and picks next to it, a beginner's music book, five formal suits, and seven white karate suits plus head gear, shin pads, fighting gloves and mouth pieces. An 8 1/2x11 picture of Siroj and Umbir sat in the middle of everything.

"Mommy, look what father got me for my birthday. Where is he?"

Shahknoza stepped in front of orchid.

"You'll see him later".

Orchid poked Shahknoza in the back.

"Ok children, we have to go because auntie has made an appointment for us. Go back to the house and we'll bring all your gifts into the house Umbir."

Orchid smacked Shahknoza on the leg.

"Why would you say that?"

Shahknoza smacked Orchid back.

"Because he will. It's all arranged. Trust me".

They carried the clothes into the main house, placed them in Umbir's room and entered the football team's SUV which took them to a park with clowns, a slide, jumping tent balloons and food. A huge sign was written in Uzbek, Russian and English, Happy Birthday Umbir and Welcome to America. The children surrounded Umbir and the clown performed a special dance and song for Orchid's son. Taking Mehruz's hand, he ran into the festivities, leaving Orchid and Shahknoza watching. Orchid rubbed the back of Shahknoza's neck.

"Thank you, Shahknoz! I love you my sister. You're the best friend ever."

Shaknoz gave Orchid a kiss, then pointed across the park.

"I helped, but you should really thank him. He put it all together. Wait before you go over".

Following Shahknoza's finger, she saw Salim, standing next to Yusuf, on crutches. They both waved and Yusuf headed towards them, leaving Salim alone. Orchid placed her hand across her heart and Salim did the same. Yusuf arrived, embraced Orchid, and sat on a bench next to them wincing.

"It's great to see you, Orchid. The years have been good to you."

Orchid could see that Yusuf's arms, neck and chest were bigger, and that his thighs were tight in the gym pants.

"And better to you".

Yusuf gave her the thumbs up sign.

"This injury is the sign I've thought about. You know how we Tatar's are, signs and meanings. This will be my fifth year and I can get all my benefits. I'm retiring after this season and I'll just be Dr. Yusuf, sports medical specialist, and I'll be home more, unless I travel with the team. My Shah Shah will like that".

Shahknoza wiggled her hips.

"Somewhat. I like to travel. I just don't like it when you're away for weeks at a time and I'm not with you. I'm too hot and I can't take it".

Orchid put her finger to her mouth and touching Shahknoza, made a sizzling sound. Orchid watched Yusuf's mouth turn downward as he looked behind her. Orchid turned to see Siroj and Iskander walking across the park, wearing dark glasses. The closer they came, the more visible the blue knot in the middle of Siroj's lower forehead, between his eyes, along with the knots on both sides of his face. Iskander walked past them but Siroj stopped, shook hands with Yusuf and continued walking to the children's play area. Umbir, seeing his father, ran from the tent accompanied by Mehruz and embraced him. Yusuf massaged Orchid's arm.

"Boys need their fathers, or some man in their life. He'll be really fortunate because he'll have three: Siroj, Salim and me".

Yusuf's words eased the weight sitting in Orchid's stomach, which Shahknoza rubbed.

"It's okay if they don't speak to me. I've worked for everything I have and everything they was given to them because of their fathers".

The three friends watched Iskander and Siroj play with the children for about an hour, then kissing them, they walked towards the three friends. Siroj handed Orchid a card as he passed. The card had his name and said chief assistant anesthesiologist at Cedars Sinai Medical Center.

The children played until darkness descended on the park. Orchid, Shahknoza and Yusuf had watched Salim entertaining the children by playing and singing songs in Uzbek and many of the children had danced and moved to his music, while others just sat and listened. As the clown and equipment staff was packing up, Salim unplugged his piano and amplifier, then looking beyond them blew two notes on his trumpet, saying danger, then walked behind the tent where he couldn't be seen. The three friends turned to see Siroj returning with a woman, both wearing doctor's coats. Shahknoz stepped in front of Orchid, then yielded to Orchid's push in the back.

"Orchid, Yusuf, Shahknoza, this is my fiancée, Doctor Dilobar Vofar."

Orchid extended her hand and the doctor gave her two limp fingers, then nodded to Shahknoza, Yusuf and spoke to Siroj in Turkish.

"Her two Tatar friends look stupid."

Shahknoza jumped in the doctor's face.

"You look stupid! You donkey faced, hussy. And you're so skinny that a strong wind would break you in two and carry you away. You stink too, from that cheap perfume you're wearing. You must have bought your degree like your flaccid fiancé, Siroj".

The doctor back stepped and tried to leave but Siroj held her arm.

"Don't go. She's ignorant"

Siroj didn't see the open handed punch coming from Yusuf who was sitting. It lifted Siroj off his feet and he landed on his back, blood seeping from both sides of his mouth.

"Never insult my wife, Siroj".

Yusuf stood without his crutches over Siroj, who covered his mouth with a handkerchief while looking up at Yusuf.

"You've made an enemy of the wrong person, Yusuf. You forget who my father is."

Yusuf stepped on Siroj's ankle.

"I know who your father is at home, but here he's nothing. Plus, noodle dick, my wife and I are American citizens and he, nor you, can't touch us".

Yusuf limped to the bench and the doctor helped Siroj to his feet.

"He's better than all of you and we'll have nothing to do with any of you. We only came here because he wants to spend the day with his son".

Shahknoza held Orchid by both arms.

"Don't do it Orchid. He won't return him to you. He's already shown you who he is. Don't trust him".

Orchid squared herself in front of Siroj and the doctor.

"No, you can't take him. He'll spend the remainder of his birthday with his sister and us. And if you hold up the divorce papers in Tashkent because of who your father is, you'll never see your children again"

Siroj's sucking lemon mouthed look made them laugh, but he surprised them by bending down and welcoming Umbir who ran past Orchid and jumped into his arms.

"Thank you for everything papa. I love you. What happened to your mouth?"

Siroj glared at Yusuf.

"That ugly, stupid man sitting there hit me because I'm here to see you and he doesn't like it. Your mother told him to do it, but I won't destroy him because it's your birthday and I don't want to make a scene. He's a bad man, Umbir, and never trust him".

The little boy looked at Yusuf with narrowed eyes, his color changing.

Orchid pulled Umbir from Siroj and squatting, held her son's face between both hands.

"Umbir, look at me. You know mommy very well and this man, as your father called him, is your uncle Yusuf. Look at him. You've seen him before and he's a famous soccer player for our country, and he's played in England and now in the U.S. He's been my friend for many years. Many many years. You know me, Umbir. You know me and you know that mommy loves you and that I'd never bring anyone bad around you. Do you believe me?"

The boy's head moved from his mother's face, upward to his father's.

"Yes mommy".

"I don't want you in the middle of anything, but listen to me. Uncle Yusuf struck your father because your father insulted his wife, and that's mean and terrible. You'd strike someone if they insulted me wouldn't you?"

"Yes mommy".

"And you believe me, don't you?"

The boy wrapped his arms around Orchid's neck and she lifted him as she stood.

"Now kiss your father goodbye and go get your sister."

Orchid leaned Umbir towards Siroj, allowing him to kiss his father, then sat her son down and watched him run towards Mehruz, wiping his eyes. Mehruz stood in front of Salim, listening to him play his trumpet, and waved to her father as Umbir joined her. Siroj laughed and took the doctor's arm.

"She's found her Bilal. She was with him before me and he did everything except deflower her. So you see what kind of woman she is. I married her as a favor to her father because no one wanted her due to her reputation. Let's go".

They walked away leaning towards each other, whispering and laughing. Orchid swung her fists in the air and kicked in the vanishing couple's direction. Shahknoza stopped her.

"Don't worry Orchid. He's just a bitter loser who's trying to impress her".

Orchid gulped down the acidic bile rising in her throat and realized that she hadn't eaten today. Shahknoza gave her a peach, some grapes, and they joined Salim, still entertaining her children with light melodies.

Orchid pressed herself against Salim and locked her arms around his neck, kissing his ear. She felt his manhood rise and his fingertips on her back. Their hearts played the same rhythm and she squeezed her legs, trying to stop the torrents of liquid drenching her panties.

"Orchid, your children are watching us."

Orchid breathed into his ear.

"I know."

Placing her hands in both pockets, she introduced Salim to her children, saying he was her closest friend when she was in college before they were born, and he'd be joining them for lunch. Umbir and Mehruz's eyes locked onto Orchid's, and then onto Salim's, as he squatted to their height, being eye to eye. The children held his gaze, then studied Orchid, and as they began to walk, held her hands.

Yusuf and Shahknoza drove them to a store/restaurant, Follow Your Heart, where they ordered meat tasting, but not meat for everyone. Yusuf raised his glass of an apple and strawberry shake with ginger, which he'd ordered for everyone.

"First we want to honor Umbir on his fifth birthday, and welcome him and Mehruz to the United States".

Orchid sat next to Salim and placed her leg against his. Salim looked at her from the corner of his eye, occasionally turning to her, but gave all his attention to Umbir and Mehruz.

"We can talk later Orchid. Your children are watching us closely. They're very perceptive".

Orchid's hand rested on Salim's thigh.

"Yes they are, and they already know how I feel about you because they've never seen me kiss, nor hug their father. I want them to feel me, and to see their mother's face with true love".

Finishing the meal, Orchid carried Mehruz to the car and Umbir walked between she and Salim to his car. Shahknoz's cackle echoed off the walls of the restaurant as they walked through the parking lot.

"Look at your little man walking between you two and staking his claim as your mother. Those men stones are showing already".

She spoke in Turkish and Umbir responded.

"My stones are bigger than my friend Hamid's who taught me Turkish, Auntie. We speak it every day. And my grandma teaches me Farsi".

The adults gulped down their laughter and walked in silence to their cars. Riding in Salim's car, Orchid turned her body to watch Umbir, whose head dipped as he fought sleep trying to watch her and Salim. Stopping at her house, Salim lowered his window and wagged his thumb. Yusuf emerged from his car, followed by Shahknoza and lifted the sleeping Umbir, who opened his eyes and looked into Yusuf's face, from the car, and allowed him to carry him into the house and up the stairs to Umbir's room. Orchid carried Mehruz to her room, and the two undressed Mehruz. Shahknoz halted Orchid after they closed Mehruz's door.

"You're walking funny and I know what it is".

Orchid covered her mouth with a bent arm.

"Is it that obvious? I feel like I need to take a quick shower."

Shahknoza slapped Orchid on the butt.

"There's no time for a shower because he's downstairs. Just do a quick wash and change those soaked panties. They must be uncomfortable."

Orchid twisted her body.

"They are. I've been worried they'd soak through my slacks. Did they?"

Shahknoza walked around Orchid.

"No, but any woman could smell the passion coming from you. Your tail's definitely up in the air, now go".

Orchid held Shahknoza's arm.

"Shahknoz, should I let him stay?"

Shahknoza ruffled Orchid's hair.

"I would. But I don't think he'll even ask, or try."

Orchid's questioning eyes spoke to Shahknoza, who motioned her hands as if she were removing her heart then made a snapping motion with them. Orchid, moving away the tears with her fingertips, struggled to her bedroom and closed the door. She emerged wearing a beige full length hand stitched Uzbek embroidered robe with slippers to match.

Walking down the stairs, Shahknoza sat on the bottom step, and pointed into the den.

"They're doing men talk. I think I heard Salim crying. Let's wait for them".

Orchid and Shahknoza faked their laughter and the voices from the den stopped. They then descended the stairs and went into Orchid's living room and she put on Harold Melvin and the Blue Notes, featuring Teddy Pendergrass singing I Miss You, and scooting next to Shahknoza, held her hand. Salim and Yusuf emerged from the den. Yusuf angled his head towards the door.

"Come my little whirlwind. I have an anatomy test in the morning. Congratulations on your new post and making it to America, Orchid. I know we'll see you soon".

Shahknoza placed her face against Orchid's while kissing her.

"Be patient with him and yourself, Orchid".

They departed, leaving Salim and Orchid alone. Salim sat next to Orchid.

"I like this song, and I'm still surprised you still have this CD".

"I have everything you ever gave to me, Salami".

His smile widened and Orchid pulled his face to hers.

"I've been waiting to do this for years. I never stopped loving you, Salim. Even though I was angry with you for the wrong reason, then angrier with myself, I never stopped loving you".

Cupping his face between her hands they devoured each other's mouths until their salty tears stopped them. Dropping her hands, Orchid rested her hand on the bulge on Salim's leg. Bending down, she kissed it, and he lifted her head.

"Wait, my love. There's nothing more I want than to love you, but I'm still afraid".

Orchid, moved off the couch to her knees and kissed his feet.

"Salim, I love you, and I'm so sorry. I'm so sorry and I hate myself for being so stupid. I just never".

He pulled her from the floor and standing lifted her into his arms.

"I know. I know, and if I'd been shown something by my family, I probably would have given it some serious thought. But that still doesn't eliminate my fear."

He lowered them to the floor, then removed both their clothes, and they lied there staring into each other's eyes until he rose and struggled into his pants, top, then left, leaving Orchid alone.

CHAPTER FOURTEEN

Orchid sat next to Shahknoza, watching the boys form a line on both sides of the dojo and adjusting their sparring helmets and gloves. Siroj and Iskander stood back-to-back in the middle of the mat, watching them prepare for the last stage of their belt test, sparring. Umbir, a head taller than the other boys his age, eyes had turned to glass and his jaws clenched and unclenched. Siroj turned to Iskander and nodded, then Iskander left the mat and called a boy's name from another room. The boy, a bit taller than Umbir, but not as broad, had a green belt. The other male students shifted and Iskander called Umbir to the mat. Orchid heard a familiar voice behind her.

"That's strange. Umbir is an orange belt and he's fighting with a green belt. Men, they always have to challenge themselves and others."

Orchid's stomach made a sound and Shahknoza, hearing it, touched her knee. Orchid noticed Mehruz peek her head from a room near the front door, and watched Umbir quickly glance at her, then hit his gloves together.

The boys bowed to Siroj, Iskander, then stepped back. The other students from all the rooms came to the doors to watch. Stepping forward, after Siroj clapped his hands, the green belt kicked with his left foot, and the kick landed against Umbir's head, knocking him down. Umbir rolled over and jumped to his feet, shaking his head. The green belt then faked with his left foot, shifted his position to his right, faked a punch with his right hand, then threw a left hand punch to Umbir's chest, knocking him flat on his butt. Red faced, Umbir took three deep breaths, slammed his back against the mat and flipped himself up to a standing position. The other students made an "Oh" sound. Orchid had seen Salim teaching Umbir that move on one of his Saturday visits when he gave her son his guitar and private martial arts classes. This was what he called his bonding time, and spent as much of the day as he could with the children. He'd converted the entire second guest house into a studio with instruments of every kind, and had written musical patterns on the walls with definitions. A piano was isolated behind a partition, and there he had patterns for Mehruz and Umbir to practice. Orchid smiled to herself, hearing him teach Mehruz to read music in groups, and to practice the left hand, then the right hand, and finally to read them together with her eyes focusing on the cluster of notes. He did the same with Umbir and the guitar, practicing the guitar with him, giving her son assignments to have prepared whenever he came by, or called, which was every day, and he had helped Orchid convert a room off the garage into a gym, complete with mirrors, mats, punching bags, and exercise equipment where he taught her children martial arts. He was always tough but tender with them, never raising his voice, and demonstrating and explaining every move with words a child could understand. They'd all eat together in the kitchen nook, not at the dining room table, and Salim would tell them stories in different languages, making everyone laugh, and afterwards they'd walk together, all four of them around the acres in back of the house, always carrying a big stick, his head moving from side to side. Once, they'd been walking and Mehruz had fallen and cut her arm. A deep gash showed,

Salim put a tourniquet on it blood had seeped out,

and before he could lift her, they were surrounded

by a pack of wolves who'd come from the darkness.

Salim had pulled the children and Orchid behind

him, then holding the stick at length and turning the

night beam on the walking light to see clearly,

moved it around until he spotted the alpha male.

Salim moved them in a circle, had told Orchid to

untie Mehruz's tourniquet, and put the blood on his

left hand. Orchid did that and Salim threw the blood

at the alpha male, splattering blood on his nose. The

alpha male, at least four feet in height, showed teeth

and circled. Salim crouched, meeting the wolf's

eyes, then raising to his full height, swung the stick

downward, the blow landing on the animal's skull

with a crack. The animal moved sideways, then

dropped to the ground, twitching. Salim hit it again,

and screaming, charged the other wolves which

fled, some fighting with each other as they ran. Picking up Mehruz and Umbir, he walked backwards holding Orchid's children, then turned and ran with them, still holding the stick and the night light. Reaching the house, he stitched Mehruz's arm, then took Umbir with him into the bathroom, where he washed her son who'd wet himself, talking to him all the time. Orchid noticed how her children asked about him coming over after that, and warmth and admiration beamed from their eyes whenever he was at their home. He read them Uzbek folk tales in English at night, and taught them Uzbek folk songs on the piano and guitar.

The flipping upwards was far advanced for a beginner, and only she, Mehruz and Salim knew that Umbir was actually farther advanced than the orange belt he wore, and though Siroj had someone pick them up every day to practice martial arts with

mostly Russian children at the dojo, he and Iskander
owned, Salim perfected what they'd learned and
never criticized Siroj and Iskander, nor commented
on the bruises on Siroj's body from being punished.

Mehruz, moving her thick shoulders with each step,
stood at the edge of the mat, and told Umbir in
Turkish the boy was left handed, before her father
Siroj lifted Mehruz and carried her to the door of
the room with the other girls. Orchid smelled
Derby, one of Salim's favorite colognes.

"Circle left."

Salim's voice in French came from the back and
Umbir nodded, staring into the green belts now
alarmed eyes. Umbir smirked, and Orchid leaned
against Shahknoza.

"He's angry now."

Umbir raised his right leg as if to kick, then extending his left arm and touching the other boy's rib cage, threw a quick right hand to the same spot, followed by a left hand, then moved up the boy's body throwing a combination of punches, a seven Salim called it because of the seven punch combination, then finished with a spinning roundhouse kick to the side with his left foot, and a reversed right spinning kick to the solar plexus, extending and stretching his leg for full power, which knocked the boy across the mat and onto his back. The boy was unconscious, his body jerking. Siroj grabbed Umbir, swinging him around because Umbir had run to the boy and raised his arm to finish the attack. A gasp tremored through the audience, and Shahknoza rose to her feet clapping.

"Yes, Umbir. That's how you show the Russians what an Uzbek boy can do. Yes".

Siroj dropped Umbir and waited for his son to bow. Umbir obliged, bowing to both his father and Iskander, then walked to the edge of the mat and bowed to Salim before returning to his group. Standing with them, Umbir slapped fives with his groupmates, and returned the blink Orchid sent him, without smiling like she did.

Yusuf and Salim joined Orchid and Shahknoza in the dojo seats. They watched the other boys spar with those wearing their same belts, the same size, then waited for the girls. Salim held Orchid's hand during the break and walked with her to a white hair and bearded honey colored broad chested man, with knife slit eyes and an oval face, who stood arm in arm with a saucer eyed, wide nosed also white haired and oval faced, tree-legged, wide hipped woman, with locks hanging to her waist. Miriam stood next to them along with Ziyod.

"Orchid this is Mr. and Mrs. Jamal and Fatima Akbar, my parents".

Orchid went to one knee and kissed both their hands.

"It is an honor to meet you Mr. and Mrs. Akbar. Salim has told me a lot about you".

The parents removed their hands from Orchid.

"Get up daughter. I understand your customs but you don't have to do that. I've been waiting to meet you for years. You're the one he allowed to break his heart and now he's happy as a bull in a barn full of heifers. A mother always wonders about that one. You're prettier than my daughter said. It's a pleasure to finally meet you. Please stand".

"Fatima."

Mr. Akbar smacked his lips.

"I'm delighted Orchid. My son and I have had many discussions about you and I'm glad we've finally met."

Orchid stood, then dropped to her knees again and placed her head against Miriam's feet.

"Please forgive me, dear Miriam. You were like a sister to me and I burned you badly by doing something terrible to you. I'm so sorry".

Miriam joined Orchid on the floor and both women ignored the people watching them and their harsh words in Russian.

"Don't do that, sister. I forgot about that years ago and I don't know, as much as I love my family, what I'd do if I were in the same position. Yes, I was angry with for awhile, but I overstood Orchid. I really did, so let's get up together, sister, and speak no more of it".

The two women rose together and Miriam used her handkerchief to clean Orchid's face. Yusuf held a shaking Shahknoza and Ziyod rubbed Miriam's back. The crying group walked into the sparring room together and returned to their seats.

The girls entered and Mehruz was called to the mat, purse mouthed. Once Iskander clapped his hands, she flew into the other girl, her eyes narrow, kicking and punching, beating the other girl across the mat and finally knocking her down and to her knees, after a right to the stomach leaving the girl trying to suck.

'That's one vicious child. Salim, you didn't lie about her. My goodness".

The child's mother called Mehruz an animal in Russian and Orchid and Shahknoza were held by Salim and Yusuf until the Russian woman and her daughter fled from the dojo. Both Umbir and

Mehruz earned their Blue belts, from Iskander and Siroj, and after receiving them, rushed to Salim, who on his knees, hugged them together.

"Thank you, Mr. Salim".

Salim rocked them, and releasing them watched as they joined their dad. Orchid, and Salim's family were turning to leave when Dilobar, the doctor hurried to her, taking her by the arm. Shahknoza stepped to the doctor but Orchid froze her with a raised hand. The doctor kissed Orchid on both cheeks.

"I want to apologize to you Orchid, Shahknoza and Yusuf. I was wrong for insulting you and I was jealous of you Orchid. I'm still jealous but I'm working with it. You see, it's you he'll always love more than me and I know it. And there are children involved and it's not good for them to feel this hostility between us. You're their mother, but I'll be like a second mother to them because of Siroj and I, and soon they'll have a little brother. Can we at least try and reach an understanding?"

Orchid looked at the long extended hand in front of her. She could feel the heat from Shahknoza's body, hear the air blowing from Shahknoza's nose and her friend sucking her teeth. Orchid took the doctor's hand and pumped it.

"Not a problem, and you're right. The children should only see harmony between us. But you must keep Siroj in check. My son could have been hurt today".

Dilobar held onto Orchid's hand.

"I told him that, but he knew what Umbir could do because Umbir showed him and like most men, he wanted to show him off. He's a proud papa".

She moved near Salim.

"Thank you Dr. Akbar. You've been wonderful to both the children".

Dr. Dilobar bowed to Salim's parents, placed her hand to her heart, nodded to everyone else, then left with Siroj, who waved to Iskander and the children. Orchid and Salim accompanied by the children, had walked to Salim's vehicle and had entered it when Orchid noticed Salim looking in the rear view mirror. He exited the SUV, with his left eyebrow raised, taking off his ring.

"Stay in the car Orchid".

Orchid turned around to see Siroj approaching the car carrying a large envelop. Salim stepped in front of Siroj, and Siroj held up the envelop and said something to Salim, who walked with him to the car and stood to the side, shielding Orchid from Siroj's right hand.

"Here are the divorce papers from home, Orchid. It's official now. We're no longer married and you're free to marry Salim and I'm free to marry Dilobar. We should both be happy now. My new son will be born in three months and my life will begin again".

He looked at Salim.

"It was you she always loved".

Salim didn't blink, and stone faced placed his back to the window blocking Orchid's view. Orchid could see his mouth move, but heard nothing until Siroj said understood and left.

Orchid rubbed Salim's face once he'd turned around with the back of her hand.

"What did you say to him my love?"

"Something between men".

Salim and Orchid followed Salim's parents, Miriam and Ziyod's, and Shahknoza and Yusuf's cars down the freeway through Westwood and into Belair. They drove through what seemed like woods and into an estate with iron gates which automatically opened. Parking the car in front of the three story home, Orchid was surprised when four men appeared and moved the cars from in front of the house. Depositing their shoes at the front door, they put on slippers and walked into the house. Orchid rubbernecked looking at the paintings and sculptures throughout the house. Shahknoza walked next to her.

"He didn't tell you about all this, did he? I was surprised too. Look at what you're going to be marrying into and they don't have their asses in the air".

Ziyod joined them as Miriam walked ahead down the houses wide marble hallway.

'She's going to get our son. It will be the first time you've seen him".

Orchid stopped in front of a young Mr. and Mrs. Akbar in white coats in a tropical setting.

"Where are they?"

Ziyod stroked Orchid's back.

"Malaysia. That's where they met. They were both in Doctors Without Borders. He's from there and she's from Venice, California, next to Santa Monica.".

"Yes, we're from different worlds, but the same tree because we're both connected to Ibrahim, or Abraham, the patriarch. Oh here's nana's boy".

Orchid turned to see a long legged and armed caramel skinned boy with a full head of walnut sized curls. He had thick eyebrows like Ziyod, Miriam's hooked nose, chiseled cheekbones and Ziyod's square chin and thick lips. His eyes were grey and Orchid looked from Miriam to Ziyod. Ziyod placed a bent knuckle across his mouth, showed his teeth and spoke to her in Turkish.

"I wondered how you'd react when you saw him. People always do and they start asking questions trying to find out if he's adopted or something because of his color. Miriam's natural mother's family were Sephardic Jews and her father's Moroccan. We met her mother and she said his grandfather had those eyes and was that color".

The three-year-old reached for Ziyod who lifted him and kissed the boy on the top of the head.

"Hello Auntie, my name is Masoud. What's your name?"

He spoke to Orchid in Uzbek.

Orchid's head jerked back.

"I'm Auntie Orchid, and these are your cousins Umbir and Mehruz".

"Oh, you're Auntie Orchid. Auntie Shahknoz talks about you all the time and so does uncle Salim. Come with me, I'll play you a song. Come on, cousins".

He slid from Ziyod's arms and taking Orchid's hand in his hand as large as hers, led her down the hall to a music room dominated by a grand piano. The tall boy guided Orchid to the piano and climbed on the stool.

"Please say your name, Auntie"

"Orchid."

The little boy listened, found the notes which made the sound of her name, then fingered two chords and played a simple melody for her.

"That's your song, Auntie. Don't forget it and every time I see you we'll sing it together. I see why my uncle loves you. You're beautiful and sweet. I love you".

He hopped from the piano stool and wrapped his arms around her legs. Orchid removed his arms and getting to her knees and at his height, hugged and kissed him, her eyes blurring. Shahknoza whimpered and Orchid could see Shahknoz brushing away the tears from her face.

"Ok Auntie, I have to go join my dad and uncles. You can go in the kitchen where grandma and my mother are".

He scuttled from the room taking Umbir and Mehruz by the hands with him, leaving Orchid on her knees and Shahknoza laughing.

"He's a prodigy Orchid, and unlike any child I've ever met. He and your children will get along perfectly. Now come, we must join Mrs. Akbar in the kitchen".

Shahknoza held Orchid's hand as they walked to the kitchen, passing Salim, Ziyod, Yusuf, and Mr. Akbar, who carried plates and platters of food into the dining room. Shahknoza entered the kitchen first.

"Mother, may I help you with anything?"

Mrs. Akbar was at the sink and didn't turn around.

"Yes, daughter. Grate those carrots for me, will you?"

Miriam was at the stove in the center of the kitchen. Orchid thought to herself that three or more families could fit inside the kitchen.

"May I help too, mother? I'd like to wash my hands first though".

Miriam and Mrs. Akbar turned around with sunshine dancing from their faces.

"The washroom's over to the right daughter. You can slice the un-chicken when you return".

Shahknoza winked at Orchid and as they walked to the washroom, she heard Miriam.

"I told you mama".

"That you did, Miriam. She's alright".

Shahknoza guided Orchid into the washroom, the size of a normal bathroom, but with only sinks.

"Shahknoz, what was that about?"

Shahknoza switched into Tatar.

"I was here when their other brother who's now in Malaysia brought his girlfriend here. She sat on the couch and tried to stay close to him all the time instead of coming into the kitchen to help out. Mrs. Akbar was cordial to her after that, but not friendly, and Khalid, that's his name, took her home after we finished eating and they split after that".

Orchid turned on the faucet.

"My mother would probably do the same. That's how women get to know each other. Remember Yusuf's mom?"

Shahknoza wiggled her fingers in the air.

"You know I do. She was the mother I never had".

Orchid's frown spoke words to Shahknoza.

"Oh, you didn't know? She died. They've really had you in their world haven't they. Welcome back".

Leaving the washroom Shahknoza told Orchid, Miriam and Salim's other two brothers were in Malaysia visiting family and recruiting nurses to come work in their clinics. The family owned six clinics in the Los Angeles area and two in the Bay Area.

Shahknoza and Orchid returned to the kitchen and Mrs. Akbar inquired about Orchid's family, though Orchid realized from her questions that she already knew about her family. Mrs. Akbar dried her hands on a paper towel and leaned against the sink.

"I've never seen my son, nor my daughter, so upset as when they returned from Uzbekistan. I know my son's in love with you and there's no one he wants to be with as much as you, but I want to say something to you, girl, and I want you to hear me clearly. If you hurt my children again, I'll hunt you down wherever you are and give you the worst homegirl ass kicking you ever had. Do I make myself clear?"

Orchid paid close attention to the veins showing in Mrs. Akbar's crossed arms.

Miriam moved and Mrs. Akbar froze her with a raised left eyebrow. Orchid had seen Salim raise his eyebrow like that.

"Yes, I understand Mrs. Akbar and I'll never do that again because I never want to lose him".

Mrs. Akbar opened her arms.

"I believe you and I can feel it. Now give me a hug daughter, and welcome to the family."

Embracing Orchid, she spoke into her ear.

"The road to heaven and hell is full of good intentions, daughter. Be vigilant".

Salim stepped into the kitchen, then backed out. Orchid heard him tell whomever was with him to wait, then peeked around the corner as Mrs. Akbar released Orchid, and reentered the kitchen followed by Mr. Akbar, Ziyod, and Yusuf. They carried the food into the dining room, sitting it on a dining room table long enough to accommodate all of them and stood behind their chairs. Orchid, Miriam, and Shahknoza walked in a line behind Mrs. Akbar, who waited while her husband pulled out her chair to the right of her, as did all the men for the women. Masoud sat to the left on his grandfather in a child's seat placed inside a chair and Umbir and Kehruz sat next to Orchid. Mr. Akbar stood after Orchid and the other women were seated.

"This is a very special celebration and I wish my other two sons were here to celebrate with us. We, as most of you know, just opened our new sports clinic, specializing in sports medicine and surgery, headed by Salim and my new son Yusuf. Let's drink to them and the clinic".

They all drank from gold rimmed glasses. Orchid tasted something which didn't smell like alcohol, but tasted like plums with a slight kick to it.

"And, they've secured contracts with all the major sports franchises, and daughter Shahknoza will be giving language instructions for all the players struggling with English. Let's drink to Shahknoza and the contracts".

Shahknoza, tomato faced, covered her eyes and Yusuf rubbed the top of her head with his first finger. They drank again and Salim stood.

"Thank you, dad! I'd like to take this moment to say how happy I am and to ask Orchid Zaynitdinova to be my partner in love for life".

He went to one knee and opened a box with a rock flanked by two obsidian stones. Shahknoza jumped from her chair.

"Say yes Orchid. Say yes. You almost lost him once so don't be stupid".

She slapped Orchid on the shoulder while speaking in Tatar. Yusuf, pulled her by the shoulders.

"Sit down Shahknoz".

Orchid stood, opened her mouth, and held the chair for support because her knees felt like ribbon. Happiness gushed from her eyes.

"I'd be honored Salim and this is what I've always wanted. Yes, yes, yes, yes".

Salim placed the ring on her finger, and standing, lifted her into the air so that their lips melted together. Mehruz, Umbir and Masoud clapped. Mrs. Akbar stood with her glass in the air.

"Welcome to the family Orchid, Umbir and Mehruz. Now you two stop that so we can eat. I'm hungry".

The evening passed with them eating, singing and dancing.

CHAPTER FIFTEEN

Orchid completed her diplomatic tasks for the day
and looked from her second-story window onto the
Miracle Mile on Wilshire boulevard in Los Angeles.
Picking up Salim's picture and kissing it, she
wiggled her toes attempting to ease the buzzing
moving from them up her thighs. The picture was
taken three days before at a reception for the Gabon
attaché she'd hosted, and they had been talking to
the attaché, speaking French, when Ziyod had taken
the picture. Salim wore a black collarless jacket as
part of his suit, and stood head-to-head with the tall
ambassador and she was next to him in a sleeveless
full length black gown, her crystal love filled eyes
looking up at him. She loved being with him in
settings like that, and introducing him as Dr. Salim
Akbar, and watching him dazzle those from the

trimmed diplomatic world with his kaleidoscopic knowledge on subjects ranging from literature, to world affairs, sports, music, and medicine if the conversation moved in that direction. They held their own as a couple, maneuvering conversations easily, supporting each other's positions, and laughing at the discomfort many displayed when experiencing an African American, in many ways, beyond them. Orchid had learned the subtleties of people's reactions to her love, which usually presented itself in people thinking Salim was from everywhere but the United States, then changing color when they found out. She realized, in those moments, that the world saw African Americans as mostly broken and damaged, and how they'd openly refer to Salim as the exception, which he'd quickly correct, calmly, with elegance and pose, giving them examples. She especially noticed an attitude by those from Africa and the Caribbean countries,

who often tried to condescend to Salim, either

through languages, or references to African

American despair, which Salim corrected, then

silenced them by referring to their country's

situations, dire existence, plight, and need for

assistance usually sponsored by African Americans

in the Congress and Senate. The diplomats' jaw

muscles would bulge, always smiling, and she knew

Salim would be a bit upset at their attitude and

words because of how he'd straighten his back and

shoulders, then spread his legs for battle.

Afterwards they'd drive to Mount Olympus, or

some secluded place, to watch the city

sparkle. They'd driven to Zuma Beach the night the

picture's been taken, listening to Duke Ellington's

Sacred Concert, then sat on the private beach where

he sang The Temptations "Firefly" to her

accompanied by the waves, then had stretched out with her on the sand, opening her reservoir with his hands. Her thoughts were sliced by the call she'd received from Shahknoza, telling her that Dilobar had delivered a ten-pound boy without complications, which caused her to sigh and wonder about her own womb which still throbbed, never having been entered by anyone but herself for years. Salim and she had laid together, slept together, their bodies crackling like logs in a fire at the closeness they shared, and they had each felt the other's juices bubbling in each other's hands, but Salim had still not ignited the flames simmering burning within her. The phone clicked and switched over and she heard the bubbles in Siroj's voice, asking her to pick up the children. Orchid held Salim's picture to her breast.

"Siroj, you're at Cedar's Sinai and Salim is there. I'd like for him to bring the children home".

Siroj's breathing was slow and easy.

"Not a problem."

Orchid called Salim who answered on the first ring.

"They're here in my office already. We'll be there in forty-five minutes".

Orchid drove to her home listening to Stevie Wonder's Songs in the Key of Life, and entered the kitchen humming *I Don't Want to Bore You.* Opening and looking into her stocked refrigerator, she thought of her aunt, and how selling her aunt's clinic, two homes, and her Mercedes had made this all possible. The phone rang and she picked it up, to Salim's voice.

"I know you don't feel like cooking, so don't worry about dinner. We'll bring something home".

It was the first time he'd said that. The first time he'd used the word home and she giggled, and danced around the kitchen doing a cha cha to Magdalena by Mr. Wonder, then went upstairs and entered the shower, allowing the jet stream to douse the flames erupting from within her. Wearing a sky blue caftan, and shoeless she sat on the couch and was awakened by Salim's kiss on her lips. Orchid looked for the children.

"Don't worry my love, they're upstairs washing up. I brought us a full meal from Follow Your Heart"

Sitting next to her, Orchid took his hand and placed it under her caftan, then maneuvered his thumb against her button. Moving she flooded his hand and Salim placed it in his mouth. Orchid pulled his mouth to hers, then stopped hearing laughter. The children, both smiling, walked hand in hand to the kitchen, and sat in the breakfast nook. They then helped Orchid set the table while Salim washed up in the bathroom. Entering the kitchen, he smelled his fingers and winked at Orchid whose face colored. Sitting at the table, and after blessing the food, they began eating until Umbir placed his fork in his plate.

'Salim, do you love my mother?"

Salim stopped chewing.

"Yes, I do".

The little boy reached for Orchid's hand.

"Mommy, do you love Salim?"

"Yes, I do son, and I accepted his ring".

Taking Salim's hand, he put it on top of Orchid's with her engagement ring.

"My dad and Dilobar got married and are happy, and now we have a little brother. Why don't you and Salim get married and then there will be two happy homes? And maybe we'll have another brother and sister"

Mehruz stood in her seat and placed her pudgy hand on top of everyone's.

"And hopefully the baby will be a boy so I can still be the only girl and he'll be tall and strong with fluffy hair and golden skin".

Orchid covered her mouth with her left hand and allowed her joy to stream down her face. They ate together as a family, joy bubbling the air, and later she joined Salim in the guest house, a red sheer nightgown under her London fog. Salim, stretched out on the bed, only his arms and the curls on his stomach leading to his chest showing.

"Please go back to the house dear, Orchid. We've waited this long. Let's stick it out, my love."

Orchid let her trench coat fall to the floor, removed her nightgown, tossing it across the room, then climbed atop Salim who gasped as she grasped his manhood and eased herself onto him.

"We've waited long enough, dear heart and there's no need to deny ourselves any more".

Salim sat upward and their arms entwined with ease.

THE END

www.ingramcontent.com/pod-product-compliance
Lightning Source LLC
Chambersburg PA
CBHW071202020726
47502CB00002B/510